THE EXTRAORDINARY JOURNEY OF
THE FAKIR WHO GOT TRAPPED IN
AN IKEA WARDROBE

ROMAIN PUÉRTOLAS

The Extraordinary Journey of the Fakir who got Trapped in an Ikea Wardrobe

TRANSLATED FROM THE FRENCH BY
Sam Taylor

VINTAGE BOOKS
London

Published by Vintage 2015

2 4 6 8 10 9 7 5 3 1

First published with the title *L'extraordinaire voyage du fakir qui était resté
coincé dans une armoire ikea* in 2013 by Le Dilettante, Paris

First published in Great Britain in 2014 by Harvill Secker

Vintage
20 Vauxhall Bridge Road,
London SW1V 2SA

www.vintage-books.co.uk

A Penguin Random House Company

Penguin
Random House
UK

global.penguinrandomhouse.com

A CIP catalogue record for this book is available from the British Library

ISBN: 9780099592952

This book is supported by the Institut Française (Royaume-Uni)
as part of the Burgess programme
(www.frenchbooknews.com)

INSTITUT
FRANÇAIS

Printed and bound by CPI Group (UK) Ltd, Croydon, CR0 4YY

For Léo and Eva, my most
beautiful creations.

For Patricia, my most
beautiful journey.

A heart is a little bit like a large
wardrobe

Ajatashatru Oghash Rathod

France

The first word spoken by the Indian man Ajatashatru Oghash Rathod upon his arrival in France was, oddly enough, a Swedish word.

Ikea.

That was what he said in a quiet voice.

Having pronounced this word, he shut the door of the old red Mercedes and waited, his hands resting on his silky knees like a well-behaved child.

The taxi driver, who was not sure he had heard correctly, turned round to face his customer, making the little wooden beads of his seat cover creak as he did so.

On the back seat of his car sat a middle-aged man, tall, thin and gnarled like a tree, with an olive-skinned face and a huge moustache. Pockmarks, the consequence of chronic acne, sprinkled his hollow cheeks. There were several rings in his ears and his lips, as if he wished to be able to zip them up after use. Oh, what a clever system! thought

Gustave Palourde, seeing in this Indian zip idea the perfect remedy for his wife's incessant chattering.

The man's grey and shiny silk suit, his red tie – which he had not even bothered to knot, but had simply pinned on – and his white shirt, all terribly creased, suggested he had been on a long flight. Strangely, however, he had no luggage.

Either he's a Hindu or he's suffered a very serious head injury, the driver thought when he considered the large white turban that encircled his customer's head. The olive-skinned face and the huge moustache made him lean towards the first of these theories.

'Ikea?'

'Ikea,' the Indian repeated, elongating the last vowel.

'Which one?' he asked, in French. Then, in stuttering English: 'Er . . . what Ikea?' Gustave was as comfortable speaking English as a dog on ice skates.

The passenger shrugged as if to suggest that he couldn't care less. *Justikea*, he said, *dontmataze-oanezatbestasiutyayazeparijan*. This is more or less what the driver heard: a series of incomprehensible babbling noises. But, babbling or otherwise, this was the first time in his thirty years spent working for

Gypsy Taxis that a customer coming out of Terminal 2C of Charles de Gaulle Airport had asked to be taken to a furniture store. As far as he was aware, Ikea had not recently opened a chain of hotels.

Gustave had heard some unusual requests before, but this one took the biscuit. If this guy had really come from India, then he had paid a small fortune and spent eight hours in an aeroplane in order to buy Billy shelves or a Poäng chair. Crikey! It was incredible, really. He had to write this encounter down in his guest book, between Demis Roussos and Salman Rushdie, both of whom had once done him the honour of placing their noble posteriors on the leopard-skin seats of his taxi. He also had to remember to tell the story to his wife that evening, during dinner. As he generally had nothing to say, it was his wife (whose luscious lips were not yet equipped with a clever Indian zip system) who monopolised the mealtime conversation, while their daughter sent misspelt texts to other young people who did not even know how to read. This would change things a little, for once.

'OK!'

The Gypsy Taxi driver, who had spent his last three weekends roaming the blue-and-yellow corridors of the Swedish store with the two afore-mentioned ladies in order to furnish the new family caravan, knew perfectly well that the closest Ikea was the one in Roissy Paris Nord, a mere €8.25 ride away. So he set his sights on the one in Paris Sud Thiais, located on the other side of the city, three-quarters of an hour from their current location. After all, the tourist wanted an Ikea. He had not specified which Ikea. And anyway, with his posh silk suit and his tie, he must be a wealthy Indian industrialist. Not likely to be short of a few bob, was he?

Pleased with himself, Gustave quickly calculated how much money the journey would make him, and rubbed his hands. Then he started the meter and set off.

What an excellent way to begin the day!

A fakir by trade, Ajatashatru Oghash (pronounced *A-jar-of-rat-stew-oh-gosh!*) had decided to travel incognito for his first trip to Europe. For this occasion, he had swapped his 'uniform', which consisted of a loincloth shaped like an enormous nappy, for a shiny grey suit and a tie rented for peanuts from Dilawar (pronounced *Die, lawyer!*), an old man from the village who had, during his youth, been a representative for a famous brand of shampoo, and who still had an impressive head of (greying) hair.

In choosing this disguise, which he was to wear for both days of his trip, the fakir had secretly wished to be taken for a wealthy Indian industrialist – so much so that he had forsaken wearing comfortable clothes (i.e. a tracksuit and sandals) for the three-hour bus journey and a flight lasting eight hours and fifteen minutes. After all, pretending to be something he was not was his job: he was a fakir. He had kept only his turban, for religious reasons.

Beneath it, his hair kept growing and growing. It was now, he estimated, about sixteen inches long, with a total population of thirty thousand (mostly germs and fleas).

Getting into the taxi that day, Ajatashatru (pronounced *A-cat-in-a-bat-suit*) had immediately noticed that his peculiar get-up had produced the desired effect on the European, in spite of the tie, which neither he nor his cousin knew how to knot correctly, even after the perfectly clear but somewhat shaky explanations of Dilawar, who had Parkinson's. But obviously this was a minor detail, as it had gone unnoticed amid the overwhelming elegance of his attire.

A glance in the rear-view mirror not being enough to contemplate such handsomeness, the Frenchman had actually turned round in his seat in order to better admire Ajatashatru, making the bones in his neck crack as he did so, as if he were preparing for an act of contortionism.

'Ikea?'

'Ikeaaa.'

'*Lequel?* Er . . . what Ikea?' the driver had stammered, apparently as comfortable speaking English as a (holy) cow on ice skates.

'Just Ikea. Doesn't matter. The one that best suits you. You're the Parisian.'

Smiling, the driver had rubbed his hands before starting the engine.

The Frenchman has taken the bait, thought Ajatashatru (pronounced *A-jackal-that-ate-you*) with satisfaction. This new look was proving ideal for his mission. With a little luck, and if he didn't have to open his mouth too much, he might even pass for a native.

Ajatashatru was famous throughout Rajasthan for swallowing retractable swords, eating broken glass made from zero-calorie sugar, stabbing his arms with fake needles, and a heap of other conjuring tricks, the secrets of which were known only to him and his cousins, and which he was happy to label *magical powers* in order to bewitch the masses.

So, when the time came to pay the bill for the taxi ride, which amounted to €98.45, our fakir handed over the only money he had for his entire trip – a counterfeit €100 note printed on just one side – while nonchalantly gesturing to the driver that he could keep the change.

Just as the driver was sliding the note into his wallet, Ajatashatru created a diversion by pointing at the huge yellow letters that proudly spelt out *I-K-E-A* above the blue building. The gypsy looked up long enough for the fakir to pull nimbly on the invisible elastic that connected his little finger to the €100 note. A tenth of a second later, the money had returned to its original owner.

'Oh, I almost forgot,' said the driver, believing the note to be nestled safely within his wallet. 'Let me give you my firm's card. In case you need a taxi for the way back. We have vans as well, if you need. Believe me, even in flatpack form, furniture takes up a lot of space.'

Gustave never knew if the Indian had understood any of what he had just told him. Rummaging in the glove compartment, he pulled out a laminated business card emblazoned with a flamenco dancer and handed it to him.

'*Merci*,' said the foreigner.

When the red Mercedes of Gypsy Taxis had disappeared – although the fakir, who was only used to making small-eared Indian elephants disappear, could not claim to be responsible – Ajatashatru slipped the card into his pocket and contemplated the vast commercial warehouse that stretched out in front of him.

In 2009, Ikea had given up on the idea of opening a branch in India, as local laws would have forced the Swedish directors to share the running of their stores with Indian managers, who would also have been majority shareholders. At the same time, the company set up a partnership with Unicef, the aim of which was to fight against child labour and slavery. This project, which involved five hundred villages in the north of India, enabled the construction of several health, nutrition and education centres throughout the region. It was in one of these schools that Ajatashatru had ended up, having been controversially fired, in his first week in the job, from the court of the maharaja Abhimanyu Ashanta Nhoi (pronounced *A-big-man-you-shouldn't-annoy*), where he had been hired as a fakir and jester. He had made the mistake of stealing a piece of sesame-seed bread, some cholesterol-free butter and two organic grapes. In other words, he had made the mistake of being hungry.

As punishment, he had first of all had his moustache shaved off, already a severe penalty in itself (even if it made him look younger), and then he had been given a straight choice between teaching schoolchildren about the perils of theft and crime, or having his right hand cut off. After all, a fakir fears neither pain nor death . . .

To the astonishment of his followers, who had become used to watching him perform all kinds of mutilation on his body (meat skewers in his arms, forks in his cheeks, swords in his belly), Ajatashatru had declined the offer of amputation and had gone for the first option.

'Excuse me, sir, could you tell me the time, please?'

The Indian jumped. A middle-aged man in track-suit and sandals had just stopped in front of him, pushing (not without difficulty) a trolley filled with at least ten cardboard boxes that only a Tetris champion, or a psychopath, could have arranged in that particular way.

For Ajatashatru, the question had sounded, more or less, as follows: *Euskuzaymoameussieuoriay-vouleursivouplay?*

It was, in other words, completely incomprehensible, and the only response it could possibly prompt was: *WHAT?*

Seeing that he was dealing with a foreigner, the man tapped his left wrist with his right index finger. The fakir, understanding this straight away, lifted his head to the sky and, as he was used to reading the time with the Indian sun, told the Frenchman it was three hours and thirty minutes later than it actually was. The Frenchman, who understood

English better than he spoke it, became suddenly aware that he was horribly late picking up his children from school for their lunch hour, and began frantically pushing his trolley towards his car.

Watching people enter and exit the store, the Indian noticed that very few customers – well, none, in fact – were dressed like he was. Shiny silk suits were apparently not in fashion. Nor were turbans, for that matter. Given that he had been aiming to blend in seamlessly, this was not a good sign. He hoped this fact would not compromise his entire mission. The tracksuit and sandals combination would have fitted the bill much better. When he got home, he would talk about this to his cousin Parthasarathy (pronounced *Parties-are-arty*). It was his cousin who had insisted he should dress like this.

Ajatashatru spent a few moments watching the glass doors open and close in front of him. All his experiences of modernity had come from watching Hollywood and Bollywood films on television at the home of his adoptive mother, Adishree Dhou (pronounced *A-didgeridoo*). It was surprising and somewhat distressing to him to see how these devices, which he thought of as jewels of modern

14

technology, had become utterly banal to the Europeans, who no longer even paid any attention to them. If there had been an Ikea in Kishanyogoor (pronounced *Quiche-and-yogurt*), he would have contemplated the glass doors of this temple of technology with the same undimmed emotion each time. The French were just spoilt children.

Once, when he was only ten years old, long before the first signs of progress had appeared in his village, an Englishman had shown him a cigarette lighter and told him: 'All sufficiently advanced technology is indiscernible from magic.' At the time, the child had not understood. So the man had explained: 'What that means, quite simply, is that things which are banal for me can seem magical to you; it all depends on the technological level of the society in which you grow up.' Little sparks had then leapt from the foreigner's thumb, before coalescing into a beautiful, hot, dazzling blue flame. Before leaving, the Englishman had given him – in return for a very strange favour which will be described in more detail later – this magical object still unknown in the small, remote village on the edge of the Tharthar Desert. And with this lighter, Ajatashatru had developed his first magic tricks, stirring the desire to one day become a fakir.

He had felt some of the same sense of wonder when he had taken the aeroplane yesterday. The journey had been an incredible experience for him. Before that, the highest from the ground he had ever flown was seven and a half inches. And even that was only when the special mechanism, cleverly hidden under his bottom during public levitations, was working perfectly. And so he had spent all night staring through the porthole of the plane, open-mouthed in amazement.

When he thought he had spent enough time in reverential contemplation of the sliding doors, the Indian finally decided to enter the store. He had travelled for more than ten hours, by bus and plane, to come here, and he did not have much time left in which to accomplish his mission. He was due to fly home the next day.

Quickening his pace, he climbed the huge staircase covered in blue lino that led to the upper floor.

For someone from a Western democracy, Mr Ikea had developed a commercial concept that was, to say the least, somewhat unusual: the dictatorial shopping experience.

Any customer wishing to reach the self-service warehouse located on the ground floor is obliged to first go upstairs, to walk along a gigantic and never-ending corridor that weaves between showcase bedrooms, living rooms and kitchens, each one more beautiful than the last, to pass a mouth-watering restaurant, perhaps stopping to eat a few meatballs or salmon wraps, and then to go back downstairs so that they can finally make their purchases in the warehouse. So, basically, someone who has come to buy three screws and two bolts might return home four hours later with a fitted kitchen and a bad case of indigestion.

The Swedes, who are very shrewd people, even thought to draw a yellow line on the floor, indicating the correct way, just in case one of the customers thinks of straying from the beaten path. The whole time that he was on the first floor, Ajatashatru did not deviate from this line, believing that the Kings of Pine Furniture had undoubtedly posted snipers on the tops of wardrobes in order to prevent all escape attempts by shooting on sight any customer overcome by a sudden desire for freedom.

It was all so beautiful that our Rajasthani, who up to this point had known only the austerity of his modest Indian dwellings, wanted to take up residence in the store, to sit down at an Ingatorp table and be served tandoori chicken by a Swedish woman in a yellow-and-blue sari, to snuggle between the Smörboll sheets on this comfortable Sultan Fåvang and take a nap, to lie in a bath and turn on the hot-water tap so he could relax a little after his tiring journey.

As in his conjuring tricks, however, everything here was fake. The book he had picked up randomly from the Billy bookcase was nothing but a plastic brick in a book jacket, the television in the living room boasted no more electronic components than an aquarium, and not a single drop of hot water (or cold water, for that matter) would ever drip from the tap in the bathroom.

Nevertheless, the idea of spending the night here began to germinate in his mind. After all, he had not reserved a hotel room, for financial reasons, and his aeroplane did not take off until 1 p.m. the next day. And all the money he had was his counterfeit €100 note, which he would need to buy the bed. And the invisible elastic would not work forever.

Relieved at knowing where he would be sleeping that night, Ajatashatru was now free to concentrate on his mission.

Ajatashatru had never seen so many chairs, spaghetti tongs and lamps in his life. Here, within arm's reach, an abundance of objects stretched out before his wonder-filled eyes. He was ignorant of the function of quite a few of them, but that hardly mattered. It was the sheer quantity that excited him. This was a true Aladdin's cave. There were objects everywhere. If his cousin had been there with him, he would have said: 'Look at that! And that! And that too!', leaping from one display to the next, touching everything he saw as if he were a little boy.

But he was all alone, so he could only say 'Look at that! And that! And that too!' to himself, and if he leapt from one display to the next, touching everything he saw as if he were a little boy, people were likely to conclude that he was a madman. In his village, mad people were beaten with long wooden sticks. He had no desire to find out if a kinder fate awaited the insane in France.

The sight of all these salad bowls and microwave ovens reminded him that he came from a very different world. To think that if he had not come here, he would perhaps never have known that such a place existed! He would have to tell his cousin all about this. If only Parthasarathy could be here too. Ajatashatru found it difficult to enjoy all these new discoveries on his own. When he was away from his family, he missed them so much that even the most jaw-dropping landscapes seemed boring and bland.

As he was thinking this, Ajatashatru arrived at the bedroom section. In front of him were a dozen beds, each arrayed with bright and colourful duvets labelled with improbable and unpronounceable names. Mysa Strå, Mysa Rönn, Mysa Rosenglim (was this some kind of word game with letters picked up randomly?). Soft and fluffy pillows, thrown on the beds in neat patterns – or, rather, placed neatly on the beds in a way that suggested they had been thrown – coaxed customers to lie down and take a nap.

A couple lay decorously on a Birkeland, their minds filled with visions of the delightful nights they would spend there together. Perhaps they would even make a child in that bed? Indeed, a sign written in French and English informed visitors that one baby in ten was conceived in an Ikea bed. Ajatashatru was pretty sure that the population of India had not been included in this statistic.

This idyllic scene was rudely shattered when two children jumped like savages onto an Årviksand and began a very loud and violent pillow fight. The young couple, lying two beds down from this battle, got up in a panic and fled towards the bathroom section, indefinitely postponing all plans for procreation.

Ajatashatru did not hang around this now-hostile environment either, and wove nimbly between the bedside tables. Not that he didn't like children. Quite the contrary, in fact. He was simply not interested in any of the models of bed on display. What he was looking for did not seem to be located in this section.

He noticed three employees, dressed in the store's colours – yellow and blue, the colours of the Swedish flag, like the sari worn by the beautiful Swedish woman who had served him tandoori chicken in his imagination – but they all seemed busy with other customers. So he went over to one of the three and waited his turn.

The sales assistant he had chosen was a short fat man wearing green-tinted glasses, diamond earrings and a toupee, the kind of person who would be caught within minutes were anyone ever to witness him committing a crime. He was busy with his computer, occasionally lifting his head to look at the customers in front of him before returning his full attention to the screen. A few minutes later, he grabbed a sheet of paper from the printer and handed it to the couple who, apparently satisfied, walked quickly away, eager to tell their friends that Sir Elton John was now working in Ikea and that he had just sold them a shoe cabinet.

After checking that the sales assistant spoke English, Ajatashatru asked him if they had the latest model of the Hertsyörbåk bed of nails on display. To illustrate his query, he unfolded the piece of paper he had retrieved from his jacket pocket and handed it to the employee.

It was a colour photograph of a bed for fakirs made of real Swedish pine, available in three colours, with stainless-steel nails of adjustable length. The page had been torn from the June 2012 Ikea catalogue, 198 million copies of which had been printed worldwide, double the annual print run of the Bible.

Several models were available: 200 nails (very expensive and extremely dangerous), 500 nails (affordable and comfortable), and 15,000 nails (very cheap and, paradoxically, very comfortable). Above the bed, a slogan boasted: *Sharpen your senses!* The price of €99.99 (for the model with 15,000 nails) was displayed in large yellow figures.

'We no longer have that model in stock,' explained the Elton John of self-assembly furniture in very good English. 'It sold out.'

Seeing the distress on the Indian's face at this news, he hastened to add: 'But you can always order one.'

'How long would that take?' asked Ajatashatru, deeply concerned at the idea that he had come all this way for nothing.

'You could have it tomorrow.'

'Tomorrow morning?'

'Tomorrow morning.'

'In that case, I'll take it.'

Pleased to have satisfied his customer, the employee sent his fingers scurrying over the keyboard.

'Your name please?'

'Mr Rathod (pronounced *Rat-head*). Ajatashatru . . . you spell it the way it sounds.'

'Oh gosh!' the employee exclaimed, stumped.

Then, more out of laziness than convenience, he wrote an X in the box while the Indian wondered how this European had known that his second name was Oghash.

'So, that's a Hertsyörbåk fakir special in real Swedish pine, with stainless-steel nails of adjustable length. What colour?'

'What are the options?'

'Puma red, tortoise blue or dolphin green.'

'I don't really see how the colours relate to the animals,' admitted Ajatashatru, who did not really see how the colours related to the animals in question.

'It's marketing,' the Frenchman shrugged. 'It's beyond the likes of us.'

'Oh. All right then, puma red.'

The sales assistant's fingers spidered frantically over the keyboard again.

'All done. You may come to fetch it tomorrow, any time after 10 a.m. Can I help you with anything else?'

'Yes, just a quick question, out of curiosity. How

come the model with fifteen thousand nails is three times cheaper than the two-hundred-nail model, which is much more dangerous?'

The man peered at Ajatashatru over the frames of his glasses, as though he did not understand.

'I have the feeling you don't understand my question,' said the fakir. 'What I mean is: what kind of idiot would buy a bed that is more expensive, far less comfortable and much more dangerous?'

'When you have spent a whole week hammering the fifteen thousand nails into the fifteen thousand holes in the wood, sir, you will no longer be asking that question. Indeed, you will regret not having bought the two-hundred-nail model, even if it is more expensive, less comfortable and more dangerous. Believe me!'

Ajatashatru nodded and took the €100 note from his wallet, being careful not to show the assistant its blank side. He had removed the invisible thread, as he would be handing the note over for good this time. The mission was about to be accomplished. Right here and right now.

'This is not where you pay, sir. You have to go

downstairs, to the tills. And you will pay tomorrow. That will be €115.89.'

Ajatashatru would have fallen over backwards had he not, at that moment, been gripping tightly to the piece of paper that the Frenchman, smiling, had handed to him.

'One hundred and fifteen euros and eighty-nine centimes?' he repeated in an offended tone.

'Ninety-nine euros and ninety-nine centimes was the promotional price. It expired last week. Look, it's written here.'

With these words, the sales assistant pointed with one pudgy finger to a line of text at the bottom of the page so small that the letters might have been ant footprints.

'Ah.'

The Indian's world collapsed around him.

'I hope you are satisfied with our service. If so, please tell everyone you know. If not, there is no need to bother. Thank you and goodbye, sir.'

At this, the young Sir Elton, considering the conversation to be over, turned his large head and his dolphin-green glasses towards the woman who was standing behind Ajatashatru.

'Hello, madame, what can I do for you?'

The fakir moved out of the way to let the lady past. Then he stared worriedly at his €100 note, wondering how on earth he could get hold of the extra €15.89 by ten o'clock tomorrow morning.

On a large sign displayed close to the tills, Ajatashatru read that the store closed at 8 p.m. on Mondays, Tuesdays and Wednesdays. So, at around 7.45 p.m. – he read the time on a plastic Swatch worn by a voluptuous blonde woman – he thought it a good idea to gravitate once more to the bedroom section.

After glancing discreetly around, he slid underneath a luridly coloured bed. Just then, a woman's robotic voice boomed from the loudspeakers. Despite the fact that he was lying down, the Indian jumped, smashing his head against the wooden slats that supported the mattress. He would never have believed it possible to jump from a horizontal position.

All his senses alert, the fakir imagined the store security guards, already in position on top of the wardrobes, pointing their sniper rifles at the Birkeland under which he was hiding, while a Franco-Swedish commando team moved stealthily and quickly to surround the bed. Inside his chest, his heart was beating to the rhythm of a Bollywood soundtrack. He undid the safety pin that held his tie in place and unbuttoned his shirt in order to breathe more easily. He feared the end of his adventure was drawing near.

After a few minutes spent holding his breath, however, no one had come to remove him from under the bed, and he deduced that the voice on the loudspeaker had merely been announcing that the store was closing.

He breathed out and waited.

A few hours earlier, just after his conversation with the sales assistant, Ajatashatru had felt hungry and headed towards the restaurant.

He did not know what time it was. And, indoors, it was impossible to calculate it from the sun's position in the sky. His cousin Pakmaan (pronounced *Pacman*) had once told him that there were no clocks in Las Vegas casinos. That way, the customers did not notice time passing and spent much more money than they had intended to spend. Ikea must have copied this technique because, although there were clocks on the walls for sale, none of them had batteries. However, whether he knew the time or not, spending more money was a luxury that Ajatashatru could not permit himself.

The Indian looked at other customers' wrists, and finally saw the time on a sporty black watch that apparently belonged to someone called Patek Philippe.

It was 2.35 p.m.

With no other money in his pocket than the €100 note that his cousin Parthasarathy had printed for him, on one side only, and which, when added to €15.89 in change, would enable him to buy his new bed of nails, Ajatashatru walked into the restaurant. His nostrils were teased by the scents of cooked meat and fish with lemon.

He went to the back of the queue, behind a woman in her forties, slim and tanned with long blonde hair, dressed in a rather bourgeois style. The perfect victim, thought Ajatashatru, as he moved closer to her. She smelt of expensive perfume. Her hands, with their burgundy-painted fingernails, picked up a plate and some cutlery.

This was the moment chosen by the Indian to take a pair of fake Police sunglasses from his pocket and put them on. He moved a little closer to the woman, and took his turn picking up a plate, a knife that did not seem likely to cut anything, and a fork with blunt prongs just like those that he used to stick in his tongue. He leaned into the woman's back and counted in his head. Three, two, one. At that very moment, feeling discomfited by the closeness of the person behind her, the Frenchwoman turned round, banging her shoulder into Ajatashatru's sunglasses and sending them flying through the air to the ground, where they smashed into several pieces. Bingo!

'MY GOSH!' the fakir cried out, staring distraught at the sunglasses before putting his plate down and kneeling to retrieve the broken pieces.

He did not wish to overdo the melodrama.

'Oh, *je suis* embarrassed!' the lady said, bending down to help him.

Ajatashatru looked sadly at the six pieces of smoky blue glass that he held in the palm of his hand as the woman handed him the gold-coloured frames.

'I am sorry. I'm so clumsy.'

Wincing, the con man shrugged, as if to say it was not important. 'Never mind. It's OK.'

'Oh, but *oui*, it minds. It minds *beaucoup*! I am going to compensate you.'

Ajatashatru clumsily attempted to put the bits of glass back in their frame. But as soon as he managed to secure one, another would immediately fall out into his hand.

As this was happening, the woman was rummaging through her handbag in search of her purse. She took out a €20 note and apologised for not being able to give him more.

The Indian politely refused. But the bourgeois lady insisted, so finally he took the note and shoved it in his pocket.

'Thank you. It is very kind of you.'

'It is normal, it is normal. And also, the meal is for me.'

Ajatashatru put the broken sunglasses in his trouser pocket and picked up his plate.

How easy life was for thieves. In a few seconds, he had just earned the €15.89 he needed to buy the Hertsyörbåk bed, plus €4.11 in pocket money. He also got a free meal (tomatoes with paprika, a salmon wrap with chips, a banana and a glass of flat Coca-Cola) and some charming company for his lunch that day. As she too was on her own, Marie Rivière (that was her name) had suggested that they eat their meal together, as well as insisting she pay for his food in return for breaking his sunglasses.

So there they were: the victim and the con man, the antelope and the lion, sitting at the same table, she shrieking with laughter at the stories told by this unusual person in a suit and turban. If someone from Kishanyogoor were to witness this scene, they would probably not believe their eyes. Ajatashatru, who had sworn a vow of chastity and chosen a balanced diet of organic nails and bolts, sitting at a table with a charming European lady while stuffing himself with smoked salmon and chips! In his village, a photograph of such an event would mean the immediate loss of his fakir's licence, perhaps even the shaving of his moustache. Probably a quick death sentence too, while they were at it.

'For some things, to be unfortunate is good,' the lady said, blushing. 'If I do not break your glasses, we do not meet. And then, I never see your beautiful eyes.'[1]

Perhaps it was not a woman's place to say that, Marie thought. Perhaps it was not for her to make the first move. But she really did think that the Indian had beautiful, Coca-Cola-coloured eyes, with sparkles in the irises reminiscent of the bubbles in the famous American soda – the very bubbles cruelly absent from the glass of Coke that Ajatashatru was currently drinking. Beautiful bubbles . . . or perhaps they were stars? Anyway, she was now at an age where, if she wanted something, she reached out

---

[1] *Author's note*: In the interests of the reader's understanding, we will polish up Marie's pidgin English during future conversations.

and took it. Life was passing so quickly these days. Here was the proof that a minor accident in a queue at Ikea could sometimes provide better results than a three-year subscription to Match.com.

The man smiled, embarrassed. His moustache pointed up at the ends like Hercule Poirot's, dragging with it all the rings that hung from his pierced lips. Marie thought those rings made him seem wild, virile, naughty . . . basically, everything she found attractive in a man. And yet his shirt was quite posh. It was an appealing mix. He looked exactly like the kind of man she often fantasised about.

'Are you staying in Paris at the moment?' she asked, trying to restrain her urges.

'You could put it like that,' replied the Rajasthani, not making it clear that he was going to spend the night in Ikea. 'But I'm leaving tomorrow. I just came here to buy something.'

'Something worth a round trip of four thousand miles . . .' she observed sagely.

So the fakir explained that he had come to France with the intention of buying the latest bed of nails to come on the market. A nail mattress was a bit like a spring mattress: after a certain time, it became worn out. The tips of the nails grew blunt, and they had to be changed.

Of course, he did not mention that he was flat broke and that his journey here (he had chosen Paris as it was the cheapest destination he had found on an Internet search engine) had been funded by the inhabitants of his native village, who, believing him to have magic powers, had hoped to help cure the poor fakir of his rheumatism by buying him a new bed. This was, in fact, a sort of pilgrimage. Ikea was his version of the grotto in Lourdes.

While he was telling her all this, Ajatashatru felt embarrassed, for the first time in his life, by his own lies. For him, not telling the truth had become second nature. But there was something about Marie that made the act more difficult. He found this Frenchwoman so pure, so gentle and friendly. He felt as if he were dishonouring her somehow. And dishonouring himself at the same time. It was rather disconcerting for him, this new feeling, this shadow of guilt. Marie had a beautiful face that shone with innocence and kindness. The face of a porcelain doll filled with that humanity which he himself had lost during his battle to survive in the hostile jungle of his childhood.

It was also the first time that he had been asked questions about his life, that someone had shown any interest in him for something unconnected with curing chronic constipation or erectile dysfunction. He even came to regret having conned Marie in such a despicable manner.

And the way she looked at him, the way she smiled at him . . . He could be wrong, but it seemed to him that she was chatting him up. This was a strange situation because in his country it was always men who chatted up women, but it made him feel good anyway.

Inside his pocket, Ajatashatru caressed the frames of his fake sunglasses. A secret mechanism enabled the six pieces of glass to interlock and be held in tension. Bang them even slightly and the pieces burst out of the frames, giving the illusion that the glasses had smashed.

Ever since he had started using this trick, he had noticed that most people felt so guilty that they gave him money as compensation for their clumsiness.

In fact Ajatashatru, who did not have an original bone in his body, had merely tweaked the famous broken vase illusion, which he had found in an old book on tricks and hoaxes.

THE BROKEN VASE TRICK

Material: a parcel, a broken vase, wrapping paper.

You walk around a large store holding a parcel covered in wrapping paper. Inside this parcel, you have previously placed the pieces of a broken vase. As you walk around the store, you spot a victim, approach her, and press your body against hers. Your sudden presence so close to her will make her jump. When this happens, you should drop the parcel. The sound it makes when it hits the floor will give the impression that the beautiful vase you were planning to give to your beloved aunt has just smashed into a thousand pieces. The victim will feel so guilty that she will instantly offer to compensate you for the damage.

'So now I know how you charm women,' said Marie with a sly little smile, 'but what I would like to know is how you fakirs charm snakes . . . That has always intrigued me.'

Truth be told, the Indian had not intended to charm the Frenchwoman, but he accepted the compliment, assuming it was a compliment. And as he felt he owed her something, having so foully cheated her of €20, he decided he would not lose face if he revealed one little fakir's secret to her. She deserved it.

'As I find you charming, in the literal meaning of the word, I will reveal to you this fakir's secret,' he told her solemnly. 'But you must swear to me that you will not repeat it to anyone.'

'I promise,' Marie breathed, her hand brushing his.

In the real world, they were separated by two plates of Swedish food, but in his mind, he took her in his arms and whispered his secrets into her ear.

Blushing, Ajatashatru pulled his hand back.

'In my village,' he stammered, 'we grow up in the presence of snakes. When I was still a baby, not even one year old, while you perhaps were playing with dolls, I had a cobra as a toy and a pet. Of course, the adults regularly checked that its glands did not contain any venom by forcing it to bite a rag that they held over an empty jam jar. The precious liquid was used to make an antidote. But believe me, even without venom, being bitten or headbutted by one of those creatures is not particularly pleasant. Anyway, you asked me how we charm snakes. The trick is this: snakes are deaf. I don't know if you were aware of that. So, the snake follows the back-and-forth motion of the *pungi*, that flute which looks like a gourd run through by a long, hollow piece of wood, and the vibrations in the air produced by the instrument. To a spectator, it looks as though the snake is dancing, whereas in fact all it is doing is following the flute's movement with its head. Fascinating, isn't it?'

Yes, Marie was fascinated. This conversation was so much more interesting than any she had shared in recent years with the young men she brought back home after a night out. How hard it is to live alone when you cannot bear solitude! It leads you to put up with so many regrettable things. And, as Marie preferred being with someone unsuitable to being on her own, the next morning was often embittered by an aftertaste of regret.

'But it is so much more difficult to charm a woman than to charm a snake,' the man added, concluding with a touch of humour.

And she smiled.

'That depends on the woman . . .' At times, the beautiful Frenchwoman seemed as fragile as a porcelain doll. The next moment, she was as bewitching as a panther. 'And on the snake . . .'

The conversation was taking an odd turn. In India, it was very simple: no one chatted up fakirs. At least, that was what Ajatashatru liked to think, as no one had ever chatted him up before. He liked this Frenchwoman a lot, he really did, but the problem was that he was here for only one night, he did not even have a hotel room, and he had not come to France in order to find a woman. He had his mission to consider and, anyway, one-night stands were not his thing. No, the best thing to do was just forget all of this now. That was quite enough of that!

'So, what did you come here to buy?' he asked, attempting to rid his mind of these ideas.

But it was difficult not to look down at the Frenchwoman's pretty cleavage and to let his imagination run riot.

'A lamp, and a magnetic rack so I can hang cutlery over my kitchen sink. Nothing very sexy.'

Taking advantage of this conversational turn, Ajatashatru opened his hand in a vertical position, palm towards him, and placed his fork there. It remained suspended in the air, behind his fingers, in a horizontal position, as if by magic.

'Or you could hang your cutlery like this,' he suggested. 'Even Ikea doesn't stock this model!'

'Oh! How do you do that?' she asked, visibly impressed.

The Indian narrowed his eyes mysteriously. He shook his hand, to show that the fork was really stuck there by a powerful and irresistible force.

'Come on, tell me!' Marie pleaded, like an impatient little girl. But each time she leaned towards him to see what he was hiding behind his hand, Ajatashatru moved further back.

In these circumstances, the fakir knew, silence would only irritate and pique the curiosity of his audience. But he had already explained the flute trick to her. If he revealed the truth behind this one too, he would effectively be admitting that everything he did was merely trickery and charlatanism. In order not to lose Marie's admiration, he preferred to do as he was used to doing with his compatriots: he preferred to lie.

'With a great deal of training and meditation.'

In fact, if Marie had been sitting next to Ajatashatru, she would have seen that the fork was trapped between the palm of his hand and his knife, which was poking out vertically from his sleeve. This, you will undoubtedly agree, requires neither much training nor much meditation.

'You haven't finished your dessert,' Ajatashatru said, to create a diversion.

In the time it took Marie to look down at her cheesecake, the Indian was able to remove the knife from his sleeve and place it, unnoticed, by the side of his plate.

'I don't like you any more,' Marie said sulkily. 'You haven't told me how you did it . . .'

'One day I must show you how it is possible to pierce one's tongue with a wire from top to bottom without leaving a hole!'

Marie thought she was about to faint. Oh, she couldn't bear that!

'Have you seen the Eiffel Tower?' she asked, to change the subject before the man got it into his head to pierce his tongue with his fork.

'No. I arrived this morning from New Delhi and came straight from the airport to Ikea.'

'There are so many fascinating stories and anecdotes about that monument. Did you know that Maupassant hated the Eiffel Tower? He ate there every day because it was the only place in Paris from which he couldn't see it . . .'

'First you have to tell me who this Maupassant is. But I do like that story!'

'He was a nineteenth-century French writer. But, hang on,' she said, pausing to eat the last bite of her dessert, 'I know an even better story. There was a crook by the name of Victor Lustig who managed to sell the Eiffel Tower. Can you believe that? After the Universal Exhibition of 1889, for which it had been built, the tower was supposed to be dismantled and then destroyed. It would have cost the French government a vast amount of money to maintain it, you see. So, this Lustig pretended to be a civil servant and, having counterfeited a national sales contract, he sold the pieces of the monument to the owner of a large scrap-metal firm for the modest sum of one hundred thousand francs.'

After Marie had converted this sum into Indian rupees, using her mobile phone, Ajatashatru felt like a novice con man in comparison with this Lustig. In order not to be outdone, he felt obliged to tell the beautiful Frenchwoman stories and tales from his own country. She laughed at the story of the fakir who was so poor he couldn't afford a nail, never imagining for a moment that the story was about him.

'Anyway,' she said finally, 'it's such a shame that you won't be able to see the Eiffel Tower. Lots of your countrymen work there, selling Eiffel Towers. Who knows, you might find one of your relatives.'

Ajatashatru did not really understand what the Frenchwoman meant by this. Perhaps something had been lost in translation. Did she mean that all the Indians in Paris were estate agents?

Had he actually gone to the Champ de Mars to verify this information, of course, he would have seen more Pakistanis and Bangladeshis than Indians, all of them busy selling (in between police patrols) key rings and other small replicas of the famous monument.

'You know, it's been a long time since I laughed like I have today,' Marie confessed. 'Or simply talked with a man about things as . . . as *different* as this. It's so good to meet someone sincere and genuine like you. The kind of person who does good and spreads that goodness around them. I feel so at ease with you. Perhaps this is a silly thing to say, but although we have just met, I have the feeling we have known each other for a long time. I must admit that I am happy, in a way, that I broke your sunglasses.'

During this speech, the beautiful Frenchwoman had once again become a little porcelain doll with long, curled eyelashes.

A sincere person who does good and spreads that goodness around him . . . Is she really talking about me? the Indian wondered, turning and looking all around to make sure she really was talking about him. And he realised that this was indeed the case. Sometimes people just have to see you a certain way, particularly if the way they see you is positive, in order to transform you into that good person. This was the first electric shock that the fakir received to his heart during this adventure.

It would not be the last.

After he had spent just a few minutes under the bed, with no one coming to disturb him, Ajatashatru ended up nodding off. The horizontal position, the darkness, the sudden silence and the long journey won out over his willpower and his tremendous physical fitness. He may have been able to pretend that he couldn't feel pain, but he was incapable of doing the same thing when it came to tiredness. And anyway, there was no one watching him here, under this bed, so he could allow himself the luxury of being weak.

When he opened his eyes again two hours later, he had forgotten where he was, as sometimes happens when one wakes up after a short sleep, and he feared he had gone blind. This fear made him jump, and once again he banged his head against the wooden slats, suddenly making him remember that he was under a bed in an Ikea store, in France, and that French beds – or, rather, Swedish beds – were much too low.

He remembered Marie, to whom he had said goodbye a few hours earlier in the bathroom section. Before they parted, he had promised he would call her the next time he came to France so they could visit the Eiffel Tower together and meet his estate agent cousins.

She had seemed disappointed that they should part in this way, and that he refused her offer to go for a drink that evening in one of the city's more lively areas. He would have liked to spend the night – his only Parisian night – with her. But that would have changed everything. It would have diverted him from his mission. This was just a quick round trip: India to France and back. If he spent the night with her, he would not be able to leave again. Anyway, at least he had her number now. Everything in his head was so muddled. Perhaps one day . . .

Ajatashatru looked to the side, but the view that extended before him consisted only of blue lino, balls of dust and bed legs. At least he couldn't see any human legs.

He slid silently out of his hiding place, glancing furtively at the ceiling in case there were any security cameras. But he saw nothing that resembled one. Then again, he didn't really know what a security camera looked like. They were not exactly common in his village. Actually, he thought, Ikea is not all it's cracked up to be: no snipers on the wardrobes, no cameras. The Soviets were much more conscientious in terms of security.

Abandoning all attempts at concealment, he walked serenely through the corridors as if he were with Marie, strolling nonchalantly between furniture displays in search of a chair or a mirror to decorate their beautiful Parisian apartment with its view of the Eiffel Tower, where Maupassant had spent most of his days in spite of his hatred of it. He imagined the Frenchwoman now, at home, alone. It really was a shame.

From his jacket pocket, he retrieved the chewing-gum wrapper on which Marie had written her telephone number. He reread the sequence of numbers over and over again until he knew it by heart. Those numbers represented love. With a sigh, he crammed the paper into the deepest recesses of his trouser pocket, close to his penis, so he would not lose it. That was where he put everything he held dear. But anyway, he had to stop thinking about her. The mission. The mission was what mattered.

Ajatashatru looked all around. How lucky he was to be here! He felt like a child who had sneaked into a gigantic toy shop. He, who had known only the modest dwellings of Adishree and his cousin Ghanashyam (pronounced *Gonna-show-'em*), now had, for one night, all for himself, an apartment of over thirty thousand square feet, with dozens of bedrooms, living rooms, kitchens and bathrooms. Although, after doing a quick calculation in his head, he had to face the fact that he would not have enough time to sleep in all the beds available to him that night.

His stomach gurgled.

Like Goldilocks in the three bears' house, the fakir – who was no more resistant to hunger than he was to tiredness, or to anything else for that matter – set off in search of a midnight feast. He entered the labyrinth of chairs in the living-room section and followed the directions for the restaurant written on the signs.

In a large grey refrigerator, he found smoked salmon, and a Tupperware box full of crème fraiche, parsley, tomatoes and lettuce. He emptied this onto a large plate, got himself a cola from the drinks machine, put it all on a plastic tray, and walked back the way he had come.

He chose a living room decorated with black-and-white lacquered furniture. On the walls, large framed sepia photographs of New York buildings provided a touch of class. He would never have found a hotel as luxurious as this for the night, particularly not for €100, or rather for a €100 note printed on only one side.

The Indian placed his tray on a coffee table, took off his jacket and tie, and sat on a comfortable green sofa. Across from him, a fake plastic television sparked his imagination. He pretended to switch it on so he could watch the latest Bollywood blockbuster while he had his smoked salmon, that strange but tasty little fluorescent orange fish, which he was eating for the second time in his life and the second time that day.

It had not taken him long to get used to luxury.

Once his meal was finished, he stood up and stretched his legs by walking around the table. It was while doing this that he noticed something on the bookcase behind the sofa that looked different from the books.

It was a newspaper – a real one – that someone must have left there. Alongside it were rows of the fake books, those plastic bricks he had seen earlier that day in other bookcases on display in the store.

As he did not speak French, he would not even have bothered opening it had he not recognised the inimitable front page of the American newspaper the *Herald Tribune*. This could be an entertaining evening, he thought. He was far from imagining just how entertaining it was going to be, though not for the reasons he expected.

Ajatashatru pretended to switch off the television and began reading the news. He could not bear the television being on when he was not watching it; where he lived, electricity was a rare commodity. He read the article on the front page. The president of France was called Hollande. What a strange idea! Was the president of Holland called Mr France, by any chance? These Europeans were decidedly odd.

And what was he to think of this former ice dancer who, each year, on the anniversary of Michael Jackson's death, moonwalked over five and a half thousand miles from Paris to the Forest Lawn Memorial Park cemetery, in a suburb of Los Angeles, where his idol was buried? Ajatashatru was no geography expert, but he found it hard to imagine how the man would continue to practise that famous dance move while crossing the Atlantic, whether he was on board an aeroplane or a ship.

Seized with a bout of nervous laughter and an irresistible urge to urinate, the Indian got up from the sofa and, in his socks, traversed the showcase living rooms – without moonwalking – in the direction of the toilets.

But he never reached them.

Voices and the sounds of footsteps coming from the main staircase suddenly broke the silence, momentarily transforming Ajatashatru's narrow chest into the stands of a football stadium during a big match. Thrown into a panic, he looked all around and then hid inside the first wardrobe he saw – a sort of blue metal, two-door luggage locker, the signature piece of the all-new 'American Teenager' collection. Once inside, he began praying that they would not notice his jacket, which he had left on the sofa a few yards from where he was hiding. He also prayed that they would not find the remains of his TV dinner on the table. Most of all, he prayed that no one would open the door of the wardrobe. If they did, he would say that he had gone inside to measure its dimensions, and that he hadn't noticed time passing. He took a wooden Ikea pencil and a metre-long Ikea paper ruler from his trouser pocket and remained motionless in the dark, expecting to be discovered from one second to the next. Inside his chest, the football supporters were smashing up their seats. Outside, the voices drew closer, and seemed to surround him. But in the end, no one discovered he was there. Perhaps it would have been better if they had.

Julio Sympa and Michou Lapaire, the manager of Ikea Paris Sud Thiais and his chief designer, climbed the stairs that led to the showcase rooms, followed by a herd of men and women in yellow T-shirts and navy cargo pants.

They were working late because they had to install a new collection.

Julio Sympa, who was six foot six and had climbed Mont Blanc four times, stopping at the top each time to read *Why I Am So Cold* by Josette Camus before going back down eight hundred and fifty-three pages later, paused in front of the 'American Teenager' bedroom and pointed in several directions before continuing on his way.

Michou Lapaire, who always wished he had been born a woman, wrote down, in a pink notebook, the furniture pointed out by his bombastic boss.

While this was happening, the members of the technical team, most of whom had undoubtedly never heard of *Why I Am So Cold* by Josette Camus nor wished they had been born a different sex, put on their gloves, unrolled the bubble wrap, and moved the crates that would be used to protect the furniture during transportation. Due to a shortage of time, the manager had given instructions not to disassemble the furniture (at Ikea! Can you believe it?) but to pack it as it was in the large wooden crates. This way, they would avoid the physically and mentally exhausting process of disassembly and reassembly.

While the technical workers busied themselves lifting up the blue metal wardrobe and putting it inside a much larger wooden crate, a gentle splashing sound could be heard, like water trickling from a tap. If one of them had opened the wardrobe, they would have seen Ajatashatru in a very unfortunate position, standing up, huddled into a corner, concentrating on giving free rein to his bladder's imagination while he was carried, rather shakily, an inch or two above the ground. It is as difficult to piss in a wardrobe as it is in an aeroplane, observed the Indian, who never would have believed that he would one day be in a position to make such an observation.

Anyway, no one opened the wardrobe door.

'When you've finished doing that, I want someone to fix that leak,' said Julio Sympa, who had excellent hearing.

Then he pointed at a bunk bed, a few yards away, as if he were sentencing it to death. Which was more or less the case.

At that very moment – in other words, at the precise instant that Julio Sympa was pointing at the bunk bed as if he were sentencing it to death, which occurred at 11 p.m. on the dot – Gustave Palourde parked his taxi by the side of the road, checked that his windows and doors were locked, and, rubbing his hands, prepared to count the day's takings.

This was his little post-shift ritual, a satisfying conclusion to a day of hard work. Ever since his wife, Mercedes-Shayana, had one day caught him, in their house (which was what they called their caravan), counting his money after a day's work, and, having found his hiding place, stolen quite a lot of the money to buy herself a crocodile calfskin bag, Gustave had got into the habit of doing it this way. Best not to tempt fate, as he told his colleagues after this incident, though what he really meant was best not to tempt Mercedes-Shayana.

Having counted his takings, the old gypsy glanced

at his notebook and noticed that the total on the paper did not correspond with the amount of money in his hands. Somewhat vexed, he recalculated several times, first in his head and then with the calculator on his mobile phone, but the result was always the same. There was a difference of one hundred euros. He rummaged through the make-up bag he had 'borrowed' from his wife (a simple act of compensation), in which he kept all his change, then he searched his wallet, and, increasingly anxious, felt around under his seat, under the passenger seat, in the glove compartment, and finally, in desperation, in the hollow around the gearstick. But all he found was dust.

One hundred euros. Gustave thought again of the green note that the Indian had given him at Ikea. That had been the most lucrative trip of the day, so he couldn't have given it to another customer in change.

'And if I don't have that damn note, then . . .'

It did not take the gypsy long to realise that he had been the victim of someone more crooked than him. He went through the scene again in his memory. The Indian handing him the note. Him taking it in his hand. Him opening his wallet and sliding it inside. The Indian waving his arms to show him something. Him looking. Him not seeing anything very interesting. Him thinking that the Indian was a bit of a loony. Him putting his wallet away. Him leaning over the glove compartment to pick up a business card.

'That toerag!' exclaimed Gustave. 'He only waved his arms about to distract me while he took his note back. *Cabrón!*'[2]

If there was one thing the Parisian taxi driver could not stand, it was being taken for a ride when he was the one giving the ride; being swindled when he should have been swindling. He swore, on his honour as a gypsy, he would find that Indian without delay and make him eat his turban.

As he did this, he stroked the little statue of St Sarah, the patron saint of gypsies, which hung from his rear-view mirror. When he drove off at top speed, she banged against St Fiacre, the patron saint of taxi drivers, who hung next to her.

For the entire duration of the journey back to his house (caravan), Gustave cursed the Indian

---

[2] *Author's note:* Spanish insult a tiny bit ruder than 'naughty boy'.

under his breath. He didn't even listen to his Gipsy Kings CD, which he always kept in the CD player. That's how annoyed he was. As he waited for a traffic light to turn green, an idea took seed in his mind. Having made his purchases in Ikea, the Indian might have used the Gypsy Taxis business card that he had given him. If so, one of Gustave's colleagues would obviously have driven him. So, all he had to do was ask where they had dropped him off, and he could go there, find him, and give him a good hiding. Without a second thought, Gustave grabbed the radio transmitter.

'Calling all units [he had copied this phrase from *Starsky & Hutch*], have any of you picked up an Indian today – crumpled grey suit, red tie pinned to his shirt, white turban on his head, huge moustache, tall, thin and gnarled like a tree . . . a Hindu, basically – from Ikea Paris Sud Thiais? This is a code T (for *Thief*), I repeat, a code T (for *Twat*). Everybody understand? That's a code T (for *waiT Till I geT my hands round your ThroaT, you filThy Indian Thief!*)

'I can't believe I trusted a *gorgio*, never mind an Indian, for a journey from Roissy to Ikea! I'll never do that again,' groaned the taxi driver, while thinking that such an event must happen about as often as the appearance of Halley's Comet (which was next expected on 28 July 2061), and that perhaps it was not such a great idea, after all, to talk about this at dinner with his wife and look like an idiot in the eyes of his daughter, who already thought he was a bit of a jerk.

A few minutes elapsed, but none of his colleagues working that afternoon said they had picked up the mysterious passenger. So, Gustave calculated, either he had used a different taxi firm, or he had hired a minivan, or he was still somewhere in the industrial zone. In the first two scenarios, he thought, there is nothing I can do until tomorrow. But for the third, I could go and see if there's a hotel near the store. I'm in the area anyway, and it'll only take me ten or fifteen minutes.

The car noisily skidded through a sudden U-turn while St Sarah pressed herself for several seconds against the body of the smiling St Fiacre.

When Gustave arrived outside Ikea, a large freight truck was leaving. He pulled to the side and let it past, blissfully unaware that inside it was a huge wooden crate which, like a Russian doll, itself contained a metal wardrobe which, in turn, contained the Indian he was looking for.

He started up again and drove around, but saw nothing suspicious. A very large and closed furniture store, a Starbucks which was open but empty . . . you could find almost anything here. Anything except a hotel. Anything except a tall, thin Indian, gnarled like a tree, in a suit, tie and turban, who conned honest French gypsy taxi drivers.

There was a residential estate on the other side of the road, but unless he knew someone who lived there, the thief could not be there.

Then again . . . thought Gustave. You could never be sure, with this kind of person. With his slick charm and his magic tricks, he might have taken refuge with one of the residents for the night.

Just in case, he drove his Mercedes through streets lined with pretty houses, losing at least five minutes in that labyrinth of homes, and came back out on the main road on which he had begun.

He had to sort this problem out as quickly as possible, because the next day he was leaving for a family holiday in Spain. So he saw only one solution: he would have to call in the professionals.

The national police's new charter for welcoming the public stated that, from now on, every French citizen had the right to file a complaint about any kind of infraction whatsoever, no matter how futile it might be, at the police station of their choice. It was the duty of the policeman, who had no rights, to register the complaint, no matter how futile he might consider it, and, in particular, not to send the plaintiff to another police station in order to get rid of him, which had been standard practice before the charter. So, for the past several months, there had been an unpleasant tension between the irate victims, fed up of waiting in queues that moved no more quickly than those at the post office or the local butcher's, and police officers embittered by the fact that they were mere humans rather than octopuses, because at least if they had eight tentacles they would have been able to type several statements at once. This tension grew even worse after nightfall, when the number of police stations open to the public diminished as quickly as an ice cube melting in Kim Basinger's navel, funnelling all the victims of crime in Paris into one single point – something the new charter was expressly intended to avoid.

No less than three hours passed between the moment when Gustave took the decision to notify the police and the moment he triumphantly signed his statement in the presence of the officer on duty.

Very concerned not to damage the harmonious relationship established by local police with the gypsy community located on the other side of the ring road, the policeman had immediately dispatched the night officer and a colleague to Ikea, accompanied by the victim, in order to inspect the video recorded by the store's security cameras during the day. They were going to find him – that damn Indian fakir who'd come here stirring up trouble with their minorities – and they were going to make him pay back what he had stolen from the taxi driver, right down to the last centime.

That was how Gustave Palourde, Police Commander Alexandra Fouliche and Police Officer Stéphane Placide came to be crammed into the store's cupboard-like control room in the middle of the night, watching a video of an Indian, fresh off the plane, spending a good twenty minutes admiring the automatic doors that led to the entrance hall, before finally deciding to walk through them.

'If he does this with each door, we'll be here until tomorrow night,' said the security guard who was controlling the video recorder.

'There aren't any more doors after this,' the store manager, Julio Sympa, corrected him, wiping his round Harry Potteresque spectacles with a thick cloth handkerchief.

'We could always watch the tape on fast-forward,' suggested Commander Fouliche, certain that such a proposal would not make her look like an idiot, in contrast to her name.

'It'll probably look like a *Benny Hill* episode,' exclaimed the taxi driver, whose cultural references were limited entirely to television.

'Shut up and let us work!' Placide interrupted him angrily. The police officer always had a hard time remaining calm.

Meanwhile, on-screen, the Indian wandered through the corridors. As soon as he moved out of shot of one camera, another picked him up. And he hadn't spotted a single one! They watched him eat in the restaurant, accompanied by a beautiful blonde woman who had bumped into him in the queue and broken his sunglasses.

'She'll end up with her legs spread,' observed Gustave, who felt as if he were watching an episode of *Big Brother* in his caravan.

They fast-forwarded through the meal, and through the man's wanderings, alone now, along the corridors. It did indeed resemble an episode of *Benny Hill*. When the Indian unexpectedly hid under a bed, they played the video at its normal speed again.

'Birkeland. Excellent choice. That's our best bed,' said Julio Sympa. Four pairs of eyes gave him dirty looks.

Next, the thief came out from his hiding place, made himself a nice snack in the kitchen, and ate it while watching a blank plastic television screen in a showcase living room. After that, he read a newspaper, sprawled out on the sofa in his socks. He could hardly have looked any more comfortable had he been at home.

'We've got him!' shouted the security guard, tapping the monitor with his index finger.

Then he jumped up from his seat like a little jack-in-the-box, rushed towards the door and left, without anyone having the faintest idea what had got into him.

The others continued to watch the recording. Around 10.15 p.m., the store manager appeared on the screen, accompanied by a small fat man who looked like he had always wanted to be a woman, and a full technical team. Julio Sympa thought he looked very photogenic and regretted not having chosen a career in film.

'But the role of Harry Potter was already taken,' he sighed resignedly, adjusting his spectacles.

They watched the Indian hop into a blue metal wardrobe before the technical team appeared and covered it in bubble wrap, and put it inside a wooden crate. The team tied the whole thing up with long straps, then carried it on a huge electric trolley to the goods lift.

At that moment, the security guard, who was a big fan of American cop shows, entered the control room. He was carrying the Indian's meal tray, which he'd found on the coffee table in the black-and-white lacquered living room. Piled on top of the tray were a grey jacket, a red tie and a pair of black shoes.

'The plate and glass are riddled with fingerprints,' he declared proudly, 'and you'll undoubtedly find some of his hair on these clothes.'

The police commander wrinkled her nose in disgust at the smelly shoes. Ignoring the security guard, she turned towards the store manager.

'What did you do with that wardrobe?'

'The wardrobe we saw on the video?' the man stammered.

'Yes, exactly. The wardrobe we saw on the video.'

'Dispatched . . .'

'Dispatched?'

'Yes, sent away. Transferred.'

'I know perfectly well what the word "dispatched" means,' snapped Fouliche, who sensed that she was being treated like an idiot. 'But where did you send it?'

Julio Sympa chewed his upper lip. If only he had been Harry Potter at that moment, he could have made himself disappear with a wave of his magic wand.

'To England . . .'

Everyone gulped at the same time.

Great Britain

Ajatashatru was woken by the sound of voices.

Loud, booming men's voices.

He had not even noticed that he'd nodded off. Since he had been in the wardrobe, he had been shaken about all over the place. He had felt himself lifted off the ground. He had felt himself moving on wheels. He had also been banged against walls, stairs and other UOs (unidentified objects).

Several times, he had been tempted to come out and confess everything. It seemed preferable to being taken on a roller-coaster ride towards an unknown destination. There was something oppressive about the combination of the darkness and the incomprehensible French voices on the other side of the wardrobe.

Nevertheless, Ajatashatru had held out.

After some time, he had no longer been able to hear or feel anything. He had wondered if he were dead. But the pain he suffered when he pinched the back of his hand had confirmed to him that he was still alive, at least for the moment, and that he had simply been abandoned to his fate in the silence and darkness. He had attempted to escape from the wardrobe, but without success. Exhausted and resigned, he must have fallen into the sweet embrace of sleep.

Now, listening to the loud voices, the Indian thought he could identify five different speakers. It was not easy – they all had the same deep, muffled tone, as if they were coming from beyond the grave – but one thing was sure: these were no longer the same voices he had heard around him in Ikea. These men spoke very quickly in a language full of onomatopoeia and sudden sharp sounds that was not unknown to him. An Arabic language spoken by black people, thought the Indian.

One of the men laughed. It sounded like a spring mattress groaning under the bouncing weight of two lovers.

The fakir held his breath, unsure whether these were the voices of friends or enemies. A friend would be anyone who was not offended by finding him in this wardrobe. An enemy would be anyone else: Ikea employees, policemen, any potential female purchaser of the wardrobe, any potential husband of the potential female purchaser coming home from work and finding a shoeless Indian in their new wardrobe.

He swallowed with great difficulty and attempted to make saliva in his mouth. His lips were sticky, as if someone had glued them together. He was filled with a terrible feeling of panic, far worse than the fear of being discovered alive: the fear of being found dead in this cheap sheet-metal wardrobe.

During his performances back home in his village, Ajatashatru went weeks without eating, sitting in the lotus position inside the trunk of a banyan fig tree, just as Siddhartha Gautama, the founder of Buddhism, had done two and a half thousand years earlier. He allowed himself the luxury of eating only once a day, at noon, and then he would only eat the rusty bolts and nails brought to him by the people of the village as offerings. In May 2005, a fifteen-year-old boy by the name of Ram Bahadur Bomjam had stolen his thunder, with the teenager's worshippers claiming that he had meditated for six months without eating or drinking. So, the eyes of the world's media had turned towards the impostor, abandoning Ajatashatru in his little tree.

In reality, our fakir loved food and could never have gone more than a single day without eating. As soon as the sun set each evening, his followers came and unrolled the canvas that hung in front of the fig tree, and he ate the food brought to him by his cousin and long-time accomplice Nysatkharee (pronounced *Nice-hot-curry*). As for the screws and bolts, they were made of coal. So, while they were not exactly delicious or digestible, they were a lot easier to swallow than actual rusty steel nails.

Ajatashatru had never fasted while locked inside a wardrobe without having food secreted in a false bottom. Perhaps he could manage it if he had to. The doctor in Kishanyogoor had once told him that no human being, even a fakir, could survive more than fifty days without food, or more than seventy-two hours without water. Seventy-two hours: in other words, three days.

Of course, only five hours had passed since the last time he had eaten and drunk, but the Indian did not know that. In the darkness of the wardrobe, he had lost all sense of time. And, as he felt thirsty right then, his hypochrondriac nature (not especially compatible with his job as a fakir) led him to believe that he had already passed the fatal deadline of seventy-two hours locked inside this wardrobe and that his life was about to be extinguished like a candle flame.

If the doctor was correct, the Indian had to drink as soon as possible. It no longer mattered if the voices outside were those of friends or enemies: this was a matter of life and death. So, our fakir once again pushed at the door of the wardrobe, attempting to escape. Once again, however, his efforts were in vain. With his puny arms, he could not – unlike his Bollywood heroes – smash open wardrobe doors. Not even Ikea wardrobe doors.

He must have made some noise, however, because the voices suddenly hushed.

Once more, Ajatashatru held his breath and waited, eyes wide open in spite of the fact that everything around him was pitch black. But he was not onstage, in a glass box filled with water, with a lid that would be removed as soon as the curtain went down. So he only held his breath for a few seconds before inhaling again with a loud, horse-like snort.

He heard a few shocked cries from the other side of the wardrobe, and then signs of agitation: a tin of food falling onto a metal floor, people pushing and shoving.

'Don't go!' he shouted, putting on his best English accent.

After a brief silence, a voice asked him, also in English, who he was. He had no doubt about the accent: the speaker was definitely African, and probably black. Then again, when one is trapped in the dark interior of a wardrobe, everyone can appear black.

The Indian knew he had to be careful. They could be animists, and believe that objects were alive, a bit like in *Alice in Wonderland*. If he did not tell them the truth, they might imagine they were dealing with a talking wardrobe and would run as fast as their legs would take them from that cursed place, taking with them his only chance of escaping from his Swedish prison. What he did not know was that these men were not animists but Muslims, and that, as they were inside a moving truck, they were not able to run for their lives, no matter how desperately they might want to.

'Very well, then, as you ask me, my name is Ajatashatru Oghash Rathod,' the Indian began, using his poshest British accent (no wardrobe could possibly have such a refined accent). 'I am from Rajasthan. You may not believe this, but I became trapped in this wardrobe while I was measuring its dimensions in a large French – or, rather, Swedish – furniture store. I do not have any food or water. Could you please tell me where we are?'

'We're in a freight truck,' said one of the voices.

'A freight truck? Well, fancy that! And is it moving?'

'Yes,' said another voice.

'Strange, I can't feel anything, but I'll take your word for it. Not that I have much choice. And would you mind telling me where we are going, if that's not too indiscreet?'

'England.'

'Well, I hope so anyway,' said yet another voice.

'You hope so? And could I possibly ask you what you are doing in a freight truck whose destination is not entirely certain to you?'

The voices conferred for a moment in their native language. After a few seconds, a deeper, more powerful voice – probably the voice of their leader – took over the conversation and replied.

The man said that his name was Assefa (pronounced *I-suffer*), and that there were six of them in the truck, all from Sudan. The others were called Kougri, Basel, Mohammed, Nijam and Amsalu (pronounce all that however you like). Hassan, having been arrested by the Italian police, was missing. The seven men had left their country – or, more precisely, the town of Juba in South Sudan – almost a year ago. Since then, they had been on a journey worthy of Jules Verne's greatest novels.

From the Sudanese town of Selima, the seven friends had crossed the border shared by Sudan, Libya and Egypt. There, Egyptian traffickers led them into Libya, first to Kufra, in the south-east, and then to Benghazi, in the north of the country. Next, they were taken to Tripoli, where they lived and worked for eight months. One night, they boarded a cramped boat with sixty other people, bound for the small Italian island of Lampedusa.

Arrested by the *carabinieri*, they were placed in the Caltanissetta refugee centre, but were helped to escape by other human traffickers, who held them elsewhere and demanded a ransom from their families. A thousand euros – an astronomical sum. The community clubbed together, and the ransom was paid. Except for Hassan, who never escaped the refugee centre.

The hostages had been liberated and put on a train that went from Italy to Spain. They ended up in Barcelona, thinking that they were in the north of France, and spent a few days there before they were able to set right their mistake by taking another train towards France, and more particularly towards Paris. So, these illegal aliens had taken almost a year to make the same journey that a passenger with the correct papers could have made in barely eleven hours. One year of suffering and uncertainty versus eleven hours comfortably seated in an aeroplane.

Assefa and his acolytes had hung around in Paris for three days before taking the train to Calais, the final stop before the United Kingdom. They spent ten days there, helped to a great extent by Red Cross volunteers who gave them food to eat and a place to sleep. This was how the police knew the approximate number of illegal aliens waiting in the zone. The Red Cross served 250 meals? Then there must be at least 250 illegals in the area.

To the police, they were illegal aliens; to the Red Cross, they were people in need. It was unsettling to live with such a duality and with constant fear in the gut.

Last night, at about 2 a.m., they had sneaked aboard a freight truck while it moved slowly in the line of vehicles waiting to enter the Channel Tunnel.

'You mean you jumped onto a moving truck?' exclaimed Ajatashatru, as if that were the only really important part of the story.

'Yes,' Assefa replied in his deep voice. 'The trafficker opened the door with a crowbar and we jumped inside. The driver must never even have realised.'

'But that's very dangerous!'

'It would have been more dangerous to stay in France. We had nothing to lose. I guess it's the same thing for you.'

'Oh, but you're completely wrong! I'm not an illegal alien, and I had no intention of going to England,' said the Indian. 'I told you: I am a very honourable fakir, and I became trapped in this wardrobe while I was measuring its dimensions in a large furniture store. I had come to France to buy a new bed of nails, and –'

'Oh, give me a break,' the African interrupted, not believing the Indian's preposterous story for a moment. 'We're in the same boat.'

'In the same truck,' the Indian corrected him under his breath.

An edifying conversation then took place between these two men, who seemed to be divided by everything, beginning with a wardrobe door, but whom fate had finally brought together. Perhaps it was easier for the illegal alien to open up to a door – a little confessional booth improvised amid the lurches of the truck – rather than having to look into the face of another man who might judge him with a frown or a blink. Whatever the reason, he began to tell the Indian everything he had felt in his heart since the day he had decided to undertake this long, uncertain journey. People like to confide in strangers.

Ajatashatru thus learned that when Assefa left his country it was not for a reason as trivial as buying a bed in a famous furniture store. The Sudanese had said goodbye to his loved ones in order to try his luck in the 'good countries', as he liked to call them. His only mistake was to have been born on the wrong side of the Mediterranean, where poverty and hunger had taken seed one day like twin diseases, corrupting and destroying everything in their paths.

The political situation in Sudan had plunged the country into an economic stagnation that had led many men – the strongest – to risk the dangers of emigration. But away from home, even the sturdiest men become vulnerable: beaten animals with lifeless expressions, their eyes full of extinguished stars. Far from their houses, they all became frightened children, and the only thing that could console them was the success of their venture.

'To have your heart pounding in your chest,' Assefa said, hitting his thorax. And a powerful sound echoed even within Ajatashatru's wardrobe. 'To have your heart pounding in your chest each time the truck slows down, each time it stops. The fear of being found by the police, huddled behind a cardboard box, sitting in the dust surrounded by crates full of vegetables. The humiliation. Because even illegal aliens have a sense of honour. In fact, stripped of our belongings, our passports, our identities, it is perhaps the only thing we have left. Honour. That is why we leave on our own, without women or children. So that we are never seen this way. So that we can be remembered as big and strong. Always.

'And it is not the fear of being beaten that twists our guts. No, because on this side of the Mediterranean we do not suffer beatings. It is the fear of being sent back to the country from which we have come, or, worse, being sent to a country we don't know, because the white people don't care where they send you – what matters for them is getting you out of their country. A black man brings chaos, you see. And this rejection is more painful than being beaten, because that only destroys the body, not the soul. It is an invisible scar that never vanishes, a scar with which you must learn to live, to survive, day after day.'

Because their will was unshakeable.

One day they would live in one of the 'good countries', no matter what it took. Even if the Europeans had no desire to share the cake with them. Assefa, Kougri, Basel, Mohammed, Nijam, Amsalu: six among the thousands who had tried their luck before them, or who would try it after them. Always the same men, the same hearts pounding inside those starving chests, and yet, in these lands where there was so much of everything – houses, cars, vegetables, meat and water – some considered them as people in need, and others as criminals. On one side the charities, and on the other the police. On one side those who accepted them unconditionally, and on the other those who sent them home unceremoniously. There was something to suit all tastes in this world. As Assefa repeated, it was impossible to live with this duality and the fear in the gut of never knowing what was going to happen next.

But it was worth it.

They had abandoned everything to go to a country where they believed they would be able to work and earn money. That was all they asked: to find some honest work so they could send money to their families, to their people, so that their children no longer had those big, heavy bellies like basketballs that were at the same time utterly empty, so that they could all survive under the sun without those flies that sat on their lips after first sitting on cows' arses.

Why are some people born here and others there? Why do some have everything and others nothing? Why do some live while others – always the same ones – have the right only to shut up and die?

'We have come too far now,' continued the

cavernous voice. 'Our families have put their trust in us, they have helped us to pay for this journey, and now they are waiting for us to help them in return. There is no shame in travelling inside a wardrobe, Ajatashatru. Because you, you understand the helplessness of a father when he cannot even put bread in his children's mouths. That is why we are all here, in this truck.'

There was silence.

This was the second electric shock that the fakir received to his heart during this adventure. He did not say anything. Because there was nothing to say. Ashamed by his own base motives, he thanked Buddha that he was on this side of the wardrobe door so he did not have to look the man in his eyes.

'I understand,' the Indian, deeply moved, managed to stammer.

'Now it is your turn, Aja. But first, we are going to take you out of there so you can drink some water and eat some food. Judging by your muffled voice, it must be a thick crate.'

'It's not because of the crate,' the Indian whispered to himself, swallowing a sob.

The fakir did not cry his eyes out, but he still felt a heavy weight descend upon his frail shoulders. It was as if he no longer lay inside the wardrobe but underneath it, crushed by the weight of revelations and remorse, of the hardness and injustice of life. In the time it took for him to be freed from his metal prison, Ajatashatru came to realise that he had been blind up to this point in his life, and that there existed a much darker and more deceitful world than the one he had seen for himself.

Life had not been a walk in the park for him. Strictly speaking, he had not had what most Westerners would call a very happy childhood or a model upbringing. First of all, his mother had died and his father had abandoned him, and then he had suffered the abuse and violence that a somewhat boisterous child can unwittingly attract in environments where only the fittest survive. He had been propelled into the ugliest and hardest kind of adult life without enjoying a real childhood. But when it came down to it, he had had a place to live and people who loved him: his cousins, and the woman next door who had raised him like her own son. He didn't know if he should include his followers in this category. In reality, perhaps, those people feared him more than they loved him. It was because of all this that he had never before felt the desire to leave his native country. He had sometimes been hungry, it was true, and he had paid dearly for that − in his case, with his moustache, because he had always managed to save his hands from amputation. But, after all, a fakir's life was supposed to be painful, wasn't it? So what was he complaining about?

As the wooden crate cracked under blows from the crowbar, Ajatashatru imagined the Africans leaping, cat-like, out of the night, and landing in the moving lorries that had brought them here. Assefa had admitted that they would slip inside the trailer of a truck while it was stopped in a lay-by at night, preferably when it was raining so that the sound of the rain would cover the sound of their movements. Ajatashatru imagined them hiding behind containers, chilled to the bone, out of breath, desperately hungry.

But all journeys have an end, even the hardest and most gruelling, and they were about to arrive at a safe harbour. They had succeeded in their mission. They were going to be able to find work and send money to their families. And he was glad to be with them as they reached the finishing line, to witness the happy ending to their courageous adventure.

'You've got to the heart of the matter, Assefa. When they don't give you what you deserve, you have to take it yourself. That is a principle which has always governed my life,' he added, without making it clear that this noble principle included theft.

The Indian had just come to the realisation that he was surrounded by the true adventurers of the twenty-first century. Not those white yachtsmen in their €100,000 boats, taking part in races and solo round-the-world trips that no one but their sponsors gave a toss about. Those people had nothing left to discover.

Ajatashatru smiled in the darkness. He, too, wanted, for once in his life, to do something for someone else.

Mohammed, the smallest of the Africans, had found, on the floor, the crowbar that the trafficker had used to open the truck's doors. In the rush, the man must have dropped it and forgotten it there, before he had jumped out of the truck.

So Nijam and Basel, the two strongest, used it to smash the hinges of the big wooden crate in which the Indian – an illegal alien, whether he liked it or not – was enclosed. Fifteen minutes later, they had dispensed with the crate and were down to the blue metal wardrobe, which looked similar to a locker in an airport or a football team's changing rooms.

'I don't know how you can still be breathing,' said Assefa, quickly stripping away the layer of bubble wrap that covered the wardrobe.

Finally the wardrobe door opened and Ajatashatru appeared, magnificent amid the fragrance of his urine.

'You look just the way I imagined you!' exclaimed

the Indian, seeing his travelling companions for the first time.

'You don't,' the leader replied bluntly, perhaps expecting to see the Rajasthani in a sari with a large knife on his belt, riding a small-eared elephant.

For a moment, Assefa contemplated the fakir who stood in front of him: a tall man, thin and gnarled like a tree. He was wearing a slightly soiled white turban on his head, a crumpled white shirt, and shiny grey trousers. On his feet were a pair of white sports socks. He looked like a government minister who'd been stapled repeatedly in the face and then shoved, fully clothed, in the washing machine. Basically, nothing like Assefa might have imagined an illegal Rajasthani migrant would look, had he ever taken the time to imagine what an illegal Rajasthani migrant might look like.

Nevertheless, the African took him in his arms and hugged him tightly before offering him a large, half-empty bottle of Evian and some chocolate bars bought in boxes of twelve at the Lidl supermarket in Calais.

Ajatashatru, panicking at the idea of dying of dehydration, grabbed the bottle and downed it as the others watched in amazement.

'You must have been locked in there for a long time,' said Kougri.

'I don't know. What day is it?'

'Tuesday,' replied the leader, the only one who knew what day it was.

'What time?'

'Two thirty in the morning,' replied Basel, the only one with a watch.

'In that case, I may have been panicking for nothing,' said Aja, giving the empty bottle back to Assefa.

Then he grabbed a chocolate bar. Just in case . . .

'All right,' said the leader. 'Now that you're here with us, and now that you've had something to eat and drink, and given that we have a good two hours, in the likely scenario that this truck is heading towards London, it's time for you to tell us your story, Aja. From the beginning. I want to know what drove you to make this journey, even if your reasons are not very different from ours.'

His voice had softened, as if confiding in the Indian had created an invisible bond between them, the beginning of a friendship that nothing now could weaken. Chewing his upper lip, the Indian wondered what he could tell his new friend . . .

apart from the truth. His people, too, had clubbed together to pay for his trip, but only because he had duped them and stolen from them for years. How could he admit to Assefa that his last trick had been to feign rheumatism and a slipped disc so that they would cough up for his plane ticket so he could buy the bed of nails, which he planned to resell at a higher price in his home village? How could he admit that to a man who had suffered during every second of his gruelling and uncertain journey?

To his surprise, Ajatashatru began to pray. Buddha, help me! he begged in his head, while the huge black man waited. It was roughly at that moment that the truck braked suddenly and the doors opened.

The first thing Ajatashatru saw in England was a blanket of white snow in the black night. There was something unreal about the scene, particularly given that it was summer. So what he had heard was true: it really was cold in this country. The North Pole was only a few degrees of latitude away, after all.

As he got closer to the open doors, however, the Indian noticed that the temperature was actually quite warm for a summer night in the Arctic, and that what he had initially taken to be snowflakes were, in fact, just polystyrene beads blown from the packaging of his wardrobe by the draught of air.

The fakir shaded his eyes with his hand. Blinding stars, which soon turned into car headlights, were pointed at him.

Turning round, he realised that he was now alone and that his Sudanese friends had all rushed behind the wooden crates, as if they were more sensitive to the light than him, vanishing totally and leaving him very conspicuous.

'Get out of the vehicle slowly!' shouted an authoritarian voice in much better English than his or the Africans'. 'And put your hands on your head!'

The Indian, who had done nothing wrong, obeyed without a word and jumped out of the trailer. There, he found himself face to face with a man wearing a large white turban, just like his. For a moment, he thought they must have put a mirror in front of him, but he didn't have to be a genius at Spot the Difference to see that it was nothing of the kind. The man was clean-shaven, in contrast to Ajatashatru, who had a large, stringy moustache and a three-day beard. He was also wearing a thick, black bulletproof vest with *UKBA* written on it in big white letters. The fakir did not know what UKBA meant, but the pistol hanging from the man's belt gave him a pretty good clue. So he decided this would be a good time to reel off the excuse he had prepared the night before. He delved into his pocket, took out the Ikea pencil and paper ruler to illustrate his words, and gave his excuse in Punjabi.

'I know, I know,' replied the policeman in the same language, clearly used to finding illegal aliens in Ikea wardrobes holding paper rulers and pencils.

Then the policeman pushed him to the side, frisked him all over through his clothes, firmly and meticulously, and handcuffed him. At the same time, four of his uniformed colleagues appeared suddenly out of the darkness and clambered into the trailer, military-style.

They soon came out again, accompanied by the six Africans, whose hands were cuffed by those Serflex straps that gardeners use to attach trees to stakes so that they grow straight.

'What are you doing with Africans?' the stunned policeman asked in Punjabi.

The fakir did not know how to reply. With fear in his gut, he just watched as his companions got inside a van marked *UKBA* – United Kingdom Border Agency – before he himself was violently shoved inside. When the truck slowed down and then stopped, he got to experience what his friend called the syndrome of the pounding heart. The 'good countries' had welcomed him in their own special way. Assefa was right: you never knew what kind of reception you were going to get. This time, however, it seemed as if the Red Cross would not be part of the equation.

In the overcrowded cell, Ajatashatru learned from an Albanian in a tracksuit and sandals that: 1) he was in Folkestone, England, a few minutes' walk from the exit (or the entrance, depending on which way you're going) of the Eurotunnel; 2) no, there was no Ikea near here; and 3) yes, he was up shit creek.

The Indian looked around him. They were all there, the men no one wanted. For Assefa and his friends, the journey had reached its end, but it was not the end they had hoped for. As he had promised himself, the fakir had been with them when they crossed the finishing line. But this was not the happy ending he had imagined for them when locked up in his wardrobe, before his new friends had kindly freed him from his metal and bubble-wrap prison, then given him food and water. Someone must have mixed up Buddha's files. This could not be the destiny of these brave men! Heaven must have made a mistake: it had sent them the wrong welcoming committee.

Ajatashatru's eyes met Assefa's, which were sad. Sitting on a concrete bench between two imposing North Africans, he appeared to have shrunk. His eyes seemed to say: 'Don't feel bad for us, Aja.'

While the fakir wove between the detainees – who made a charming mosaic of colours, accents and odours, all in tracksuits and sandals – heading towards his travelling companion so he could offer him words of comfort, the Indian policeman who had arrested him one hour earlier, whose name was Officer Simpson, opened the Plexiglas door behind which all the prisoners were held like fish in a waterless aquarium, and told Ajatashatru to accompany him to his office.

'Get ready for a rough fifteen minutes!' said the Albanian, for whom this was his tenth attempt to enter Great Britain.

But, confident that his good faith and the policeman's understanding nature – he had the same blood as the fakir, after all – would clear up this terrible mix-up for good, Ajatashatru cheerfully followed in his compatriot's footsteps.

'Let's be clear about this: I am not your

compatriot,' said Simpson, in English this time, as if he had read the fakir's mind.

He told him to sit down.

'I am a British citizen and a government employee. I am not your friend,' he added, just in case there was any further doubt. 'And I am certainly not your brother or your cousin.'

He's more royalist than the king, this one, thought Ajatashatru, coming to the realisation that his good faith and the policeman's understanding nature would certainly not be enough to clear up this terrible mix-up. You are only here today because your parents took a trip in the trailer of a truck one day, between crates of Spanish strawberries and Belgian cauliflowers, thought the Indian, deciding not to share these feelings with the man in question. Your parents undoubtedly experienced the fear that attacks the gut every time the truck slows down and stops.

Impervious to these thoughts, the policeman typed a few words on his keyboard, then raised his head.

'So we're going to start again at the beginning, and you're going to explain the whole thing to me.'

Officer Simpson asked for his name, his parents'

names, his place and date of birth, and his occupation. The response to the last question prompted
open disbelief.

'Fakir? That still exists, does it?' he said, his face
creased with scepticism and contempt. Then he
pointed to the sealed transparent packet that lay
on the desk.

The Indian immediately recognised his personal
effects.

'This is what we found on you. Take a good look
and sign here.'

With these words, the policeman handed him a
sheet of paper on which each object was listed:

- 1 Gypsy Taxis business card from Paris, France
- 1 chewing-gum wrapper with *Marie* and a
  French mobile phone number written on it
- 1 genuine Indian passport with a genuine
  short-term visa for the Schengen Area
  provided by the French Embassy in New
  Delhi. Entry stamp dated 4 August at Roissy
  Charles de Gaulle Airport, France
- 1 page from the Ikea catalogue advertising the
  Hertsyörbåk model of bed of nails
- 1 imitation leather belt

- 1 pair of Police sunglasses, in six pieces
- 1 poor-quality counterfeit €100 note, printed on one side only, attached to a 20cm length of invisible thread
- 1 legal €20 note
- 1 wooden pencil and 1 one-metre paper ruler, both marked Ikea
- 1 half-dollar coin with two identical faces

'Why did you take my belt?' asked the Indian, intrigued.

'So you couldn't hang yourself with it,' Officer Simpson replied curtly. 'We also systematically remove shoelaces, but you didn't have any. Could you tell me why you don't have any shoes, by the way?'

The fakir looked at his feet. His sports socks were no longer very white.

'Because I left them in the Ikea store last night, when I had to hide in the wardrobe so that the employees wouldn't see me . . .'

Having spent the last nine years uncovering illegal aliens in the most improbable hiding places and listening to their bullshit all day and all night, Officer Simpson did not believe a word of the story told by this Ajatashatru 'Oh gosh' Rathod (though he doubted that was his real name), just as he had not believed a word spoken by the leader of the Sudanese illegals when he interviewed him earlier.

'All right, seeing as you're not even trying, I'm going to cut this short. We searched your boyfriends, the Jackson Five, and guess what?'

Ajatashatru guessed that Officer Simpson had failed maths, because there had in fact been six Sudanese men in the truck with him. But he thought it better not to say this.

'We found several pieces of evidence on them,' Officer Simpson continued, 'that suggested you had all stayed in Barcelona. Given what the weather's like down there, I have to wonder why you come and give us grief in England. You know it rains all the time here, don't you? Monsoon season has nothing on this.'

'Listen, I know you are trying to discourage me, and I thank you for all this useful information you've given me about the weather in your delightful country. And one day, I would love to come back here, as a tourist, in less unfortunate circumstances. But I can assure you that I never intended to come to England and that I do not know those Sudanese fellows.'

'Sudanese? Ha, there you go!' exclaimed the policeman, proud of having caught the criminal red-handed in a lie. 'So you know more than I do. Your boyfriends didn't tell me anything. They even refused to divulge their nationality. Anyway, we're used to it. Most illegal aliens destroy or hide their passports so we can't identify their nationality and send them back where they came from.'

'But I told you where I come from. That proves I am not an illegal alien.'

'Your visa is valid only in the Schengen Area, and let me remind you that England is not, and never will be, in the Schengen Area. So, by definition, you are an illegal alien. Dress it up all you want.'

Annoyed by this, the Indian explained once again the reasons why he had come to France, and his idea (not quite so brilliant as it had first seemed, clearly) of sleeping in Ikea so that he could be there the next morning to buy his bed of nails: the Hertsyörbåk special fakir model made in real Swedish pine, puma red in colour, with stainless-steel nails of adjustable length. He pointed out that he had put his order in yesterday, and that there was surely some record of that on the store's computers, and that it would be a good idea to check with Ikea Paris.

As he said this, he pointed to the transparent packet on the desk, but realised as soon as he did so that the Ikea order form given to him by Elton John was actually in the pocket of his jacket, which had remained in the store.

Officer Simpson sighed. 'All right, I've heard enough. I'm going to take you back to the cell, and the removal team will take you to the airport early tomorrow morning.'

'The airport? Where are you sending me?' Ajatashatru demanded, his eyes full of fear.

'We're sending you back where you came from,' said the policeman, as though this were obvious. 'You and your boyfriends are going back to Barcelona.'

In the pockets of the Sudanese men, the British authorities had found receipts from Corte Inglés, a large department store in Barcelona. The immigrants had bought six cans of beer there, plus a packet of peanuts and two boxes of chocolate-covered doughnuts. This was all the UKBA's officers needed to repatriate the crooks, in accordance with international readmission agreements, to the illegal aliens' last known country of stay – in this case, Spain.

In this way, some illegals are sent back to the country they have just travelled from, in application of the Chicago Convention, while others, more rarely, are sent back to their country of origin. Back to square one.

In this particular case, the police knew perfectly well that the truck they had stopped was coming from France, because they had caught it on its way out of the Eurotunnel. For that reason alone, they could have sent the immigrants to eat their peanuts and their chocolate-covered doughnuts in the country of the frog-eaters, whose border was like a sieve. That would have taken an hour at most and would have cost nothing, or very little.

However, repatriating them to Spain, even if it was more expensive for the state, had considerable advantages for the British authorities, who had been trying for some time to send illegal aliens as far as possible from their borders. They knew perfectly well that such people would, as soon as they were free, make another attempt to enter the United Kingdom. If they could have built a giant catapult capable of propelling the immigrants thousands of miles away, they would have put them all in it without a moment's hesitation.

'An aeroplane chartered by the aviation police is going to take you back to Barcelona,' the policeman informed him, and then terminated the interview.

So it was that, a few hours later, as the sun was looming on the horizon, the fakir found himself on the windy runway of a small airport in Shoreham-by-Sea, near Brighton, on the south coast of England.

If you squinted, it was possible to see, on the other side of the Channel, the bluish, evanescent outline of the land of the Gauls.

The bluish water.

The bluish sky.

The bluish seagulls.

The bluish faces of illegal aliens.

Or, at least, that was what Aja saw through the smoky, bluish lenses of his sunglasses, which he had pieced back together. They had been returned to him, along with the rest of his personal effects, firstly because he no longer represented a threat to himself or to others, and secondly because he would soon be free. They had even given him back his counterfeit €100 note, judging that it was so badly printed (and on only one side!) that nobody could possibly be fooled by it.

The fakir was sitting on an aeroplane, no longer handcuffed, between an asthmatic Moroccan and a flatulent Pakistani. Curious to know precisely what kind of fire he was likely to land in, having been thrown from the frying pan, and also to pass the time, the Indian asked his dear companions a long list of questions about Barcelona. What was there to see? What was there to do? Could you swim in the sea at this time of year? Was there a monsoon season? What was a doughnut? Oh, and did they have an Ikea?

But none of these questions were answered. Not because the two illegal aliens did not feel like chatting – quite the contrary – but because neither of them had ever set foot, or even the tip of their little toe – in Barcelona, or even in Spain.

The Pakistani had arrived in Europe via Brussels Airport, carrying a fake Belgian passport, and reached England hidden in a truck, between two pallets of cabbages. But the British authorities had found a fan on his person (he could not stand the smell of cabbages) and that was all they needed to decide that he had come from Spain, because everyone knew that only the Spanish still used that old-fashioned, manual form of ventilation.

As for the Moroccan, he had entered the Schengen Area from Greece, having first been all over the Mediterranean basin. He had crossed the Balkans, Austria and, finally, France, hidden in the false floor of a Greek tourist coach. But the English had found a small wooden spoon in his pocket, the handle of which had broken off during the journey. A British agent who had just been to Seville on his holidays believed this was part of a pair of castanets, and the Moroccan's fate was instantly sealed. Off you go, mate, back to Spain!

'What about you?' asked the Pakistani. 'What did they find on you?'

'Nothing.' Ajatashatru shrugged. 'They just happened to find me in a freight truck with some Sudanese fellows who were coming from Barcelona.'

He turned round and pointed at the six black men sitting in the fourth row.

'So, if I understand correctly, of the three of us, none came from Barcelona,' said the Moroccan.

'I doubt we're the only ones like that on this aeroplane,' concluded the Pakistani.

'If all you need is a guitar or a moustache for the English to suspect you of coming from Spain, then yes, I have a feeling you're right about that . . .'

He pointed discreetly at a man in the same row as them who wore a thick brown moustache and a black canvas hat.

'My friends, just think of this as a free holiday paid for by the Queen!' declared a thick Russian-accented voice from somewhere behind them. 'They put me on this frigging aeroplane because I rolled my rrs!'

Somewhere in the pile of rubbish at the local dump, next to which the Palourde family had set up camp, a rusty alarm clock announced it was 8 a.m.

'By this time, he should be in England,' muttered Gustave. He was sitting at a camping table, a million miles from imagining that the object of his thoughts was at that very moment 20,000 feet above him, stuck between an asthmatic Moroccan and a flatulent Pakistani, on an aeroplane flying south at terrific speed.

As he spoke, he caressed the sharpened blade of his Opinel knife. His only consolation was that the *gorgio* was travelling in the trailer of a heavy goods vehicle, locked inside a wooden crate without food or water. With a little luck, the thirst would slowly kill him, like a rat in a trap. It was a shame, though – he would have liked to deal with him personally, making him suffer very, very slowly.

Something moved inside the caravan.

His wife Mercedes-Shayana appeared on the doorstep in a flowery dressing gown. Then it was the turn of their daughter, Miranda-Jessica, to show her face, which was plastered in make-up and crowned by her blonde, dishevelled hair.

'You went out again last night!' said Gustave reproachfully, pointing a threatening finger at his daughter. 'I'd told you to stay in the house [the caravan] because you needed to rest. Look at the state of you now!'

'I don't care, as long as Kevin-Jésus doesn't see me like this. Anyway, I'll sleep on the plane.'

'Oh great, so Kevin-Jésus is back on the scene,' said her father sarcastically. 'I thought it was all over with him?'

Miranda-Jessica just yawned in reply.

'You're like a broken record, Gus. Leave the kid alone.'

The mother had just sat down at the little camping table and was pouring herself some of the coffee her husband had made when he got up. She put down the Thermos and buttered a slice of toast for Miranda-Jessica, who sat next to her.

'Anyway, you two had better get off your arses

unless you want us to miss our plane!' shouted the taxi driver, getting to his feet and stalking off to warm up the car's engine.

Twice a year, in an unchangeable ritual, Gustave Palourde, his wife and their daughter would leave the family house (caravan) to go on holiday. The first trip was to the gypsy festival in Saintes-Maries-de-la-Mer. Each 24 May since the Middle Ages, the gypsies had reunited in the Camargue to celebrate their patron saint, Sarah, the wax statue of whom, crying golden tears, they carried to the seaside church. More than a pilgrimage, this gathering allowed them to see friends from the diaspora who were scattered all over the world. Some of them came from more than two thousand miles away to take part in the event. The Palourde family had a seven-hour drive in Gustave's taxi, fitted out especially for the occasion. For a few years now, they had been going without their caravan (house), spending the night in the home of their cousins, whom they had known as children, lost touch with, and then reconnected with later.

For Gustave and his wife, it was the most exciting event of the year. For their daughter, it was the exact opposite, a heartbreaking nightmare. Firstly, because it meant she had to leave her current lover, and she was always afraid that, in her absence, he would find someone prettier than her, even though there were no gypsy girls prettier than her. Secondly, because long processions featuring thousands of gypsies dressed in black, weeping and yelling under the burden of a statue weighing several hundred pounds, was not necessarily the kind of activity designed to appeal to a teenage girl. And, what's more, the long black dresses and veils did not suit her at all. She had never liked Madonna's style. She was much more into the flashy, quirky style of Lady Gaga. Her only consolation was that she was able to go to the arenas at night and cop off with the young men taking part in the Toro Piscine[3] or the blunted-horn bull races.[4]

The second event of the year happened in early August – now, in other words. Gustave took a week off and they caught a plane to Barcelona to spend the money they had worked hard all year to earn. They owned a real brick house there, which had previously belonged to a great-uncle who, towards the end

---

[3] A game where bulls are ridden through a swimming pool.
[4] The bulls wear balls or champagne corks on their horns, so that the participants are not injured.

of his life, had no longer been able to bear the dampness of caravans.

Miranda-Jessica did not have to be dragged, kicking and screaming, to Barcelona. There was no lack of nightclubs and boys in the Catalan capital. She knew the hottest venues off by heart – those in the Maremagnum, the Barrio Gotico and the fantastic Port Olímpic, where she would stay up all night, shaking her booty to her favourite songs.

Which is why, on this particular morning, missing the plane was unthinkable. So the teenage girl drank her chocolate milk down in two swallows and got up to change in the caravan. She squeezed herself into a pair of faded denim shorts consisting of a few square inches of material, put on a yellow bikini top, six-inch heels decorated with diamanté, and emerged carrying a large handbag under her arm. She would take a shower that afternoon, on Barceloneta Beach.

Her mother would do the same. But it was inconceivable for her not to apply a fresh layer of make-up. So Mercedes-Shayana plastered some foundation on her face, spread Rimmel on her lashes, and smeared fuchsia-pink lipstick over her lips. She did not remove her flowery dressing gown, as she thought it was very summery and Spanish and therefore perfect for the occasion, but added some pink Lycra leggings and a pair of beach sandals.

'What a beautiful bevy of women!' exclaimed Gustave, shoving the luggage into the boot of his car.

Then he got behind the steering wheel, making the little wooden beads of his seat cover creak as he did so.

Bees and Snakes

Some problems have Daddy's name written all over them. For instance, my kids recently discovered bees had moved into a crack in our concrete front porch. So, armed with bug spray, I went out to do battle.

I got stung. Five times.

I don't like being stung by insects. But better me than my kids or wife. Taking care of my family's well-being is at the top of my job description after all. My children recognized a need, and they asked me to address it. They trusted me to protect them from something they feared.

In Matthew 7, Jesus teaches that we too should bring our needs to God (V. 7), trusting Him with our requests. To illustrate, Jesus gives a case study in character: "Which of you, if your son asks for bread, will give him a stone? Or if he asks for a fish, will give him a snake?" (VV. 9–10). For loving parents, the answer is obvious. But Jesus answers anyway, challenging us not to lose faith in our Father's generous goodness: "If you, then, though you are evil, know how to give good gifts to your children, how much more will your Father in heaven give good gifts to those who ask him!" (V. 11).

I can't imagine loving my kids more. But Jesus assures us that even the best earthly father's love is eclipsed by God's love for us. ❧

ADAM HOLZ

> **TODAY'S READING**
> **Matthew 7:7–11**
>
> If you, then, though you are evil, know how to give good gifts to your children, how much more will your Father in heaven give good gifts to those who ask him! Matthew 7:11

Father, thank You for loving us so much more than even the best father here ever could. Help us to do as Jesus said with everything that's on our hearts; to ask, seek, and knock in our relationship with You.

We can rely on our Father for everything we need.

Hope in Grief

When I was nineteen, one of my close friends was killed in a car accident. In the following weeks and months, I walked each day in a tunnel of grief. The pain of losing someone so young and wonderful clouded my vision, and at times I even felt unaware of what was going on around me. I felt so blinded by pain and grief that I simply could not see God.

> TODAY'S READING
> **Luke 24:13–32**
>
> **Then their eyes were opened and they recognized him, and he disappeared from their sight.** Luke 24:31

In Luke 24, two disciples, confused and brokenhearted after Jesus's death, didn't realize they were walking with their resurrected Teacher Himself, even as He explained from Scripture why the promised Savior had to die and rise again. Only when He took bread and broke it was it revealed that this was Jesus (VV. 30-31). Although the followers of Jesus had faced death in all its horror when Jesus died, through His resurrection from the dead God showed them how to hope again.

Like those disciples, we might feel weighed down with confusion or grief. But we can find hope and comfort in the reality that Jesus is alive and at work in the world—and in us. Although we still face heartache and pain, we can welcome Christ to walk with us in our tunnel of grief. As the Light of the world (JOHN 8:12), He can bring rays of hope to brighten our fog. 🌱 *AMY BOUCHER PYE*

Lord God, thank You for being the light in the darkness.
Bring hope when I'm sad and confused,
and help me to see Your glory.

Though we grieve, we have hope in Jesus.

The bells of the church clock tower situated opposite the police station announced it was 8 a.m.

'By this time, he should be in England,' muttered Police Commander Alexandra Fouliche, sitting at her desk.

All the same, she was not going to ask a judge for an international arrest warrant because a taxi driver had been conned out of €100. She would look like an idiot. And you know how much she hated the thought of that. She would rather have paid the man back his €100 from her own pocket and preserved her dignity.

So the police commander closed the file on Gustave Palourde, Gypsy Taxis, and threw it into the graveyard of abandoned cases, a large drawer like those you see at the chemist's, where it joined 150 other cases fit only to disappear from the face of the Earth. After that, she stood up and went to join the others at the coffee machine.

Walking past the two-way mirror that they used for identifications ('line-ups', as they called them on American TV shows), she thought she had aged overnight. Large dark rings shadowed her eyes like two parentheses that no longer had the strength to stand straight. This job is slowly eating me alive, she thought. I need a holiday.

Spain

Walking past the floor-to-ceiling windows of the arrivals lounge in Barcelona Airport, Ajatashatru thought he had aged overnight. Large dark rings shadowed his eyes like two parentheses that no longer had the strength to stand straight. This trip is slowly eating me alive, he thought. I need a comfortable bed.

He no longer looked even remotely like a wealthy Indian industrialist. He now had the shop-soiled appearance of an illegal alien and he understood why the policeman who had interrogated him had not believed his Ikea story. He would have thought the same thing, in Officer Simpson's place.

The large digital clock on the wall of the arrivals lounge indicated that it was exactly midday. Above all, the fact that he was in the arrivals lounge indicated his freedom. The Spanish immigration services, when he was taken to see them by his British escort, had barely even looked at his papers.

As his passport was in order, they had grudgingly pointed him, along with three other lucky passengers, towards the nearest exit.

The clock also indicated that, at this time, Ajatashatru should have been at Roissy Charles de Gaulle Airport, nearly seven hundred miles from here, waiting for the aeroplane that would take him back to India, with a new bed of nails in his luggage.

But all of that belonged to his old life.

While he walked through the brand-new Terminal 1 towards the baggage claim area – an obligatory trip even for those without suitcases – the Indian swore that from now on, he would not do anything else illegal. He thought about what Marie had said to him. *It's so good to meet someone sincere and genuine like you. The kind of person who does good and spreads that goodness around them.* He thought again of the story of Assefa, the leader of the Sudanese Jackson Six, whom he had just left in the passport control area with Kougri, Basel, Mohammed, Nijam and Amsalu (they did not have passports and would be there for a while yet). The two men had parted with an emotional hug, each wishing the other good luck on their journey. '*Mektoub*,' Assefa had said. 'It was written. We were meant to meet.'

The North Africans were going to try to enter Great Britain again. They believed in their promised land just as the first colonists had believed in America when they saw its coastline on the horizon. They would go back up through Spain, across France, and stop in Calais to wait for passage to England, hidden between crates of onions or cabbages.

'What about you? What are you going to do?' Assefa had asked him.

'Me? I don't know yet. I'll probably visit Barcelona, seeing as I'm here. Even though I don't have any money.'

He decided not to tell his friend that he was going to try to become a good person, that his life had changed, and that he too now wanted someone to help and to provide for.

He also kept to himself his thoughts about Marie and the crazy plans that were taking seed in his mind.

As incredible as it may seem, it was with these thoughts of love, compassion and fraternity filling his head that our fakir found himself face to face with the Parisian taxi driver whom he had conned the day before, nearly seven hundred miles from here. The man was arm in arm with what appeared to be two prostitutes and was staring at the Indian with a desperate desire to kill him.

The first thing Gustave Palourde did when he came face to face with the Indian was stare at him with a desperate desire to kill him.

'*Gorgio*, I knew I would see you again one day!'

The taxi driver was not even momentarily surprised to see the Indian here, in Barcelona, though only three hours earlier he had imagined him in England, still trapped like a rat in the trailer of a truck on its way towards the most northerly latitudes of the globe. Gustave was naturally impulsive, and his anger often overwhelmed his logical and analytical abilities.

There was no need to be a mind-reader (although Ajatashatru excelled in that particular discipline) nor to speak French (in this case, the difficult-to-comprehend French of an irate gypsy) in order to understand that our fakir ought not to hang around the area very long. But he did not have time to move a muscle.

'I'm going to kill you!' yelled Gustave, who wanted to kill him.

Saying this, he smashed him in the head with the

ice cooler he had just taken from the baggage carousel.

'I love his pierced lips!' exclaimed his daughter, who had never been allowed to pierce her lips.

'Who is he?' asked his wife, who was seeing this man – a turban on his head, olive-skinned face, huge moustache, tall and thin and gnarled like a tree – for the first time in her life.

Quickly realising that he was not a family friend, she joined forces with her husband and bravely hit the stranger in the ribs with her very full crocodile calfskin bag.

Ajatashatru, surprised by the sudden attack mounted on him by these amateur Gipsy Kings, had not been able to evade the fifteen-pound ice cooler, which banged into his cheek, nor the crocodile bag, which struck him in the ribs. Naturally skinny, he was projected like a wind-blown feather onto the baggage carousel for a flight coming from Majorca. For a brief moment, he lay there motionless, more out of strategy (playing dead) than pain (although, now you mention it . . .), between a pushchair and a mountain of boxes of *ensaïmadas* (you don't know what that is? Neither did he). But when he opened his eyes – very carefully, in case the gypsy was waiting for him to do that before smashing him in the face with the ice cooler again – the Indian realised that he had played dead for slightly too long.

Just like Alice, the fakir had passed through to the other side of the looking glass – or, to be more accurate, the baggage depot. The machine that vomited bags had swallowed him like a common suitcase that had already been around the carousel, unclaimed by anyone.

His face burned with pain.

Gingerly, he touched his cheek. A multitude of tiny ice crystals, probably thrown from the ice cooler at the moment of impact, had lodged in the scars left behind by the chronic acne that had ravaged his face when he was a teenager.

The left half of his face was numb and frozen, as if he'd been smashed in the face with an ice cooler, which was in fact the case, or as if he'd been hit by an iron that had been left too long in a very cold room, which is, I acknowledge, a very odd analogy.

Goodness gracious! he thought suddenly. Because while it was true that he had managed to escape the madman and his harpies, there was perhaps worse yet to come.

Indeed, he now found himself in the secure (and thus forbidden) zone of a major European airport, which was not the best way of keeping his promise to return to the straight and narrow.

If any police had passed by at that moment, they would have seen a poor man's Aladdin who had swapped his magic carpet for a baggage carousel. And if the Spanish had been as competent and efficient as their English counterparts, as soon as they had overcome their shock, Aladdin would have found himself – before he had time to say 'Phew', and in accordance with the same international re-admission agreements that had caused him to be sent here – somewhere between the North Pole and Iceland, for the good and simple reason that he had been discovered with little ice crystals embedded in his cheeks.

So, like a criminal seeking to rid himself of damning evidence, the fakir vigorously rubbed his face with the sleeve of his shirt while the carousel continued to carry him along its meandering path into the depot.

Tom Cruise-Jesús Cortés Santamaría had spent the past five minutes looking at himself in the rear-view mirror of the little red-and-yellow golf cart belonging to the airline company Iberia.

Though he was only twenty-eight, he thought he had aged overnight. Large dark rings shadowed his eyes like two parentheses that no longer had the strength to stand straight. This job insecurity is slowly eating me alive, he thought. I need a permanent contract.

As he was about to drive back into the baggage depot, a man carrying an ice cooler strode towards him. He was accompanied by a woman in a flowery dressing gown who looked like she had just got out of the bath and a teenage girl dressed like those professionals he saw by the side of the road on his way to work.

'Señor, my suitcase has been eaten by the

machine,' said the man in fluent Spanish with the hint of a French accent.

Having decided not to let the Indian escape him this time, this was the only excuse Gustave had come up with to enter the secure zone of the baggage depot. His large beer belly and lack of physical fitness prevented him jumping onto the carousel and following his enemy directly.

'Just wait a bit, it'll come back out,' the baggage handler replied, tired of always having to respond to the idiotic requests of passengers whenever he was unlucky enough to find himself on this side of the terminal. 'The carousel goes round in circles.'

'I know, I know . . .'

'But if you know, then why –'

'Yes, but the problem is that my daughter is hypo!' the Parisian taxi driver improvised, having seen that his plan A was not going to work.

'Hyper? She looks pretty calm to me. Not to mention very pretty.'

Flattered, Miranda-Jessica gave a shy smile and bowed her head, her cheeks aflame. The young Spaniard was very handsome in his blue uniform. Almost more handsome than Kevin-Jésus.

'Not hyper – hypo!' the gypsy corrected him, shouting to demonstrate the urgency of the situation. 'Hypoglycaemic! My daughter is diabetic! She needs a GlucaGen injection straight away to get her blood sugar levels back up! And the GlucaGen is in the suitcase!'

He had always wanted to replicate an episode of *E.R.*, his favourite American TV series. The long-awaited day had finally arrived.

'She doesn't look sick,' replied the baggage handler, unfazed by the man's exigent demeanour.

Gustave elbowed Miranda-Jessica, who immediately lifted up her head and put on the most pain-filled expression she could manage.

'OK, I'm going,' said the baggage handler, who preferred to give in to the tourist's demand rather than stay there and talk about it.

And, anyway, the girl was very cute.

He started up his golf cart.

'I'm coming with you. You don't know which suitcase it is,' said Gustave truthfully, placing the ice cooler on the floor and his large backside on the passenger seat.

Tom Cruise-Jesús Cortés Santamaría looked for a moment at the person sitting next to him: a small man, in his fifties, wearing cheap black trousers with darts and a black shirt. A large gold chain (the kind that are used to moor yachts) and a thick carpet of salt-and-pepper chest hair could be seen in the V at the top of his shirt. Had it not been for the ice cooler and the way the two women looked, the young man would have bet that this Frenchman was on his way to a funeral.

And then it hit him.

'Are you *gitano, hermano*?' he asked, almost certain of the answer.

'Well, yeah!' replied Gustave, as if this were obvious, wiggling his thick fingers covered in gold rings. 'Of course I'm a gypsy.'

'Well, why didn't you say so?' said Tom Cruise-Jesús Cortés Santamaría, suddenly cheering up. He, too, wiggled his long fingers covered in gold signet rings, as if this were a secret code they shared.

Then he raced his turbo-charged golf cart through the terminal. He was always first in line when it came to saving a pretty, young gypsy girl.

Overcome by curiosity, Ajatashatru had opened one of the mysterious cardboard boxes that were piled up next to him on the carousel and labelled, in pretty red-and-gold lettering, *ensaïmada mallorquina*.

To his surprise, it turned out to be a sort of large brioche, its shape somewhere between that of a snail and Princess Leia's hairdo, its circumference more or less the same as a 33rpm vinyl record.

He took a bite. It was delicious. The cake was a bit floury and stodgy, but accompanied by a little water it would have been fine. The problem was that he didn't have any water.

As he wondered how people could check in mountains of brioches as ordinary luggage, and how the baggage handlers could load them in the aeroplanes without eating a couple, he heard the purr of a car's engine.

In an agile movement, he leapt from the carousel.

It was high time, anyway, as the carousel was about to take him back to the other side of the terminal, where the Parisian was undoubtedly waiting for him with his deadly ice cooler.

A quick glance to the left, a quick glance to the right. Nothing. Nothing except for that brown leather trunk, as big as a fridge, that was passing a few yards from him on a carousel going in the opposite direction. Without a second's thought, he jumped on it. As luck would have it, the trunk was not padlocked. He unzipped it while looking back over his shoulder. A little red-and-yellow golf cart was coming towards him. The driver and the passenger, whose face he couldn't see properly, seemed not to have noticed him.

Inside the trunk was a portable wardrobe full to the brim with clothes. A wardrobe! Aja thought, his eyes glimmering with disbelief. He grabbed armfuls of the clothes and their hangers and threw them in a pile behind the carousel. There were elegant dresses, expensive lingerie, elaborate and well-stocked make-up bags. This probably belonged to someone important, or rich, or both.

The fakir got into the trunk, half an *ensaïmada* in his hand, just in case, and zipped it shut from inside. He had never been in such a big trunk in his life. He did not have to dislocate his shoulder, as he usually did when he was preparing to get inside his magic box. He exhaled. At least no one would be skewering this box with long, sharp swords. Well, not unless the Frenchman got his hands on it . . .

While the plebs continued to file between the seats to take their places on the aeroplane, like a centipede in Bermuda shorts and sandals, Sophie Morceaux, who had been the first to board, was already sipping from a glass of cheap champagne in the second row.

A passing Italian, speaking very loudly and waving his arms around, sent a minuscule particle of dust flying into one of the beautiful actress's green eyes. In touching her eye to remove the irritating dust, she accidentally dislodged her contact lens, which instantly disappeared in the jungle of blue carpet on the floor.

The young woman spent several minutes kneeling on the floor, between two chairs, scratching around in the wool fibres with her long, slender fingers, until a stewardess finally came along to help her. The result was no better, however, and Sophie Morceaux was forced into the horrifying realisation:

she was now one-eyed. Which was unbearable, I'm sure you'll agree, for an actress who had not even been in *Pirates of the Caribbean*.

While the passengers moved towards their places, the stewardess swam against the tide like a salmon and spent a minute or two on the gangway in discussion with a woman wearing a fluorescent yellow vest and large headphones over her ears and holding a walkie-talkie.

They absolutely had to find Sophie Morceaux's Vuitton trunk and bring her the toiletry bag from the outside pocket.

Luckily, it had not yet been loaded on the aeroplane. At the bottom of the gangway, the chief baggage handler explained to the woman with the walkie-talkie that the trunk was being given special treatment, in view of its owner (it was not every day that you had the famous and beautiful actress Sophie Morceaux in your aeroplane) and was therefore not travelling with the rest of the suitcases in the large metal AKH containers. He then pointed to a beautiful, brown Vuitton trunk, the size of a small refrigerator (22 x 50 x 22 inches), perched on a trolley.

The Spanish woman rummaged around in the

outside pocket of the trunk, took out a matching toiletry bag, and zipped it back up again. This was the first time she had ever seen such a luxurious piece of luggage. With her miserable salary, and in these lean times of economic crisis, she knew she would never be able to buy anything like it. She could barely even afford the toiletry bag, in fact.

'OK, we're done,' she told the chief baggage handler, who, aided by two other men, loaded the trunk into the only heated, ventilated and pressurised baggage hold on the aeroplane.

If, in the dark depths of that trunk, sandwiched between a pair of knickers and a piece of *ensaïmada*, Ajatashatru had called for a genie, the genie would have said to him, in a voice as deep as Barry White's: 'Fakir, I have some good news and some bad news for you. The good news is that you have been put in the only heated, ventilated and pressurised baggage hold on the aeroplane, which means you will not have turned into an ice cream by the time you arrive at your destination. The bad news is that you will never see Barcelona, because you have just been loaded in the hold of an aeroplane that is taking off shortly for an unknown destination. Here we go again!'

The scene had only lasted a few minutes, but when Gustave Palourde and Tom Cruise-Jesús etc. etc. entered the baggage depot, the Indian had disappeared.

Gustave, who felt bad about lying to a fellow gypsy, had told the baggage handler the truth as soon as he got in the golf cart. And the truth was that he wanted to beat the shit out of the foreigner who had conned him out of €100. The young Spaniard, for whom blood ties were the most sacred of all and who never missed an opportunity to beat the shit out of somebody, rallied to the cause of his blood brother without any further explanation. Besides, he had been relieved to find out that the pretty teenage girl, who was not diabetic, was also not in any danger.

And so, excited by this impulsive manhunt, the two gypsies drove through the labyrinthine corridors in search of the Indian who had once offended one of them.

Gustave no longer had his ice cooler to hand, but in his pocket he was caressing the ivory handle of his beloved Opinel knife, which he had joyfully recovered from his luggage after disembarking from the aeroplane. If the thief did not pay him back what he owed him, plus interest, he would not hesitate to put so many holes in him that he could be used as a sieve.

The two men had soon examined the whole of the carousel inside the depot, but still without discovering any trace of the crook. A baggage handler walked past them, and the young Spaniard asked him if he had, by any chance, seen an Indian, tall, thin and gnarled like a tree, with a moustache and a white turban on his head.

'The only Indian I can see is him!' replied the man, pointing an accusatory finger at Gustave. 'What is he doing here? He's not allowed on this side.'

'I know, I know, but we're looking for a suitcase containing a Gluco . . . um, sugar for his daughter, who's having a fit,' the young gypsy lied.

'Oh, I see . . .' Then a few seconds later: 'But hang on, what does all that have to do with the Indian?'

Tom Cruise-Jesús did not know what to say. But

he did realise that he would never be given his permanent contract if he got mixed up in crazy adventures like this. So he backed off.

Just as he was about to accompany the Frenchman to the passenger zone and forget this whole unhappy episode, his eye was caught by a pile of clothes that had been thrown to the floor near one of the baggage carousels.

More out of professional conscientiousness than suspicion, he stopped his golf cart and went to pick up the clothes. They turned out to be elegant ball gowns and some rather enticing sexy underwear in a size 8, which made him imagine that their owner was probably not too ugly.

'What is all that?' asked the taxi driver, who had gone over to join him.

'I don't know. It looks like someone threw all this away without really looking at it. These are some nice threads. I'm pretty sure they must belong to someone rich, or important, or both. Definitely a woman, anyway, and probably not an ugly one, if you want my opinion.'

'Where are those bags going?' Gustave interrupted him, pointing to the luggage that continued to move along the carousel.

The baggage handler went over to look at a passing pushchair and read on the green-and-white label attached to it:

'FCO.'

'FCO?' Gustave repeated, uncomprehending.

'Those bags are going to Fiumicino Airport, in Rome.'

As soon as the engines roared and the aeroplane took off, Ajatashatru realised that: 1) he was in an aeroplane; and 2) the suitcase in which he had hidden had not just arrived, as he had thought, but was about to depart.

For someone who had never travelled before this adventure, it seemed the fakir could now do nothing else. Travel broadens the mind, according to the famous saying. At his current rate of progress, Ajatashatru's mind would soon be so broad that his head would no longer fit inside the wardrobes and trunks which had, so far, been his means of conveyance.

He had been in Europe for twenty-four hours, but it seemed like an eternity. He had already set foot in France, England and Spain. And by tonight, he would be somewhere else again. Was Buddha going to condemn him to being an accidental illegal alien for the rest of his life? Or would he finally be allowed to stay this time?

He had no idea. He just hoped the aeroplane wasn't going to New Caledonia. He could not imagine spending the next thirty-two hours crammed inside a four-foot trunk with nothing but half an *ensaïmada* to eat.

At least he wasn't upside down. That would be unbearable. The trunk lay on its side, which was conducive to getting some sleep, even if he had his knees in his mouth. He hoped that this trunk would not become his coffin. A beautiful Vuitton coffin.

Because, while it was true that he wished to be buried – unlike other Hindu fakirs who continued the age-old tradition of cremation – he would prefer his death to be postponed as long as possible. He had told Marie, during their meal, about his wish to be buried. You never knew. If a terrorist carrying a bomb had blown the Ikea cafeteria to smithereens and Marie had survived, at least she would have been able to grant the poor Indian's last wish.

'I would rather be cremated, personally,' the Frenchwoman had told him. 'I'm too afraid of waking up inside a coffin.'

'And waking up in an urn wouldn't scare you?' the fakir had retorted.

The idea that he might die without ever seeing

Marie again haunted Ajatashatru's mind. He remembered her smile, her beautiful hands, her face like a porcelain doll's. He promised himself that he would call her as soon as he arrived at his destination, wherever that might be.

Let me survive, he prayed, and I will become a good, generous and honest man, just as she imagined me.

At that very moment, Buddha replied with a sleepy bark.

There was a dog in the baggage hold. And to judge from its plaintive whining, it was not a frequent flyer.

With his agile fingers, Ajatashatru searched blindly for the little mechanism that he had engaged when he closed the trunk after getting inside. If he had been able to close it from the inside, then he ought to be able to open it in the same way.

A few seconds later, he burst from the suitcase like an overripe banana escaping its skin. As luck would have it, there were not so many bags in the hold that his exit was blocked. Finally free, he stretched his legs for a while, massaging his lower back and his calves. One Indian airline used the slogan 'Travel with us and we'll treat you like a (holy) cow'. After travelling in the baggage hold of an aeroplane, locked inside a trunk, the fakir understood that the concept of a cow might not have the same meaning in every country.

The Indian stood up, but the ceiling of the hold

was far too low for someone of his size, and he was obliged to double over. So he decided to crab-walk in the direction of the whining. Crab-walking towards a dog struck him as rather original.

As it was pitch black in the hold, Ajatashatru felt his way forward. Each time he came upon an obstacle – one of those UOs (unidentified objects) – he pushed it out of the way or moved around it, depending on how heavy it was.

Soon he arrived in front of two glistening eyes, which looked at him unblinking through the darkness. He liked animals. He was not afraid of them. No one who spent their early childhood cuddled up to a pet cobra is likely to be afraid of any other animal, and certainly not a dog, man's best friend.

Ajatashatru held out what was left of the *ensaï-mada* towards the cage.

'Nice doggy, nice doggy,' he said, just in case the animal preferred the taste of human flesh to that of brioche.

He felt a large, cold, wet tongue, with a texture like veal escalope, greedily licking his fingers.

The dog's whining ceased. It seemed just as soothed by the piece of *ensaïmada* as by this unexpected company.

'Do you happen to know where we're going? Because I have no idea. I don't even know if we're going south, north, east or west, if we're flying over sea or mountains. And I'm also slightly illegal. Although I doubt whether I'll feel that fear in my gut when the aeroplane slows down and comes to a halt. The European police don't actually stop and search planes mid-flight, do they?'

The dog, apparently clueless on this subject, did not reply.

In the darkness of the hold, the power of the Indian's senses had increased tenfold, just as they had when he was trapped inside the wardrobe during the journey on the truck to England. To his great displeasure, one of those heightened senses was his sense of smell. The filthy animal stench made his nostrils quiver, but he then realised that it was not coming from the cage in front of him. He was the one who stank. Although he was not resistant to tiredness, hunger or thirst, our fakir was highly resistant to showers. Sometimes he would go several weeks without taking one. While it was true that, for the last two days, washing himself had been impossible, he could easily have done so on any of the five days preceding his trip.

But he had not even wiped his face clean. The last time he had felt water on his head, it had been rainwater. And it doesn't rain very often in the Tharthar Desert!

Siddhartha Gautama, the Buddha, had meditated under the bodhi tree for seven weeks. Had *he* taken showers?

As he had time, and as no one was going to disturb him here, Ajatashatru crouched on the metal floor of the hold in the lotus position, facing the dog's glistening eyes, and began to meditate on his new life – the life of a good, generous and honest man which awaited him at his next port of call. He had given the dog some *ensaïmada*, but that in itself was not enough to constitute a complete change. So, who could he help? And how?

The fakir had often wanted to write.

He did not lack for ideas. He had a very active imagination, and his eventful life probably helped too. In any case, that unbounded imagination had served him well when it came to inventing magic tricks that made the unreal real and the impossible possible.

He had never set his stories down on paper, though. Perhaps the act of writing was more complicated than he thought, as he had always put off attempting it.

But maybe that time was now at hand? Maybe the honest and lucrative activity he was seeking in order to kick-start his new life was that of a writer? Not a public writer . . . No, he could not imagine himself sitting on the pavement, a typewriter strapped to his chest, waiting for a passer-by to commission him to write a love letter. No, he was more ambitious than that. He wanted to write best-sellers. Well, it was a more reasonable expectation than dancing the foxtrot or being a jockey. And if it didn't work out, he could always sell Eiffel Towers in Paris.

'What do you think, my friend? Should I try to become a writer?'

The dog barked three times.

Ajatashatru took that as meaning: 'I think that's a great idea, mate. Go for it!'

On the cover there would be an old-fashioned yellow car with the word *TAXI* painted on the side, speeding through the streets of New Delhi. There would be two people. The driver: a big, bearded man with unkempt hair. And a young man on crutches, running in front of the taxi, and running very fast in spite of his handicap.

Ajatashatru smiled in the darkness.

The mad taxi driver was clearly a fictionalised version of the Parisian gypsy with his ice cooler, while he himself was the cripple crossing the street.

The title would be something like *God Takes a Taxi*. Now that he had the cover and the title, the fakir was ready to begin his novel. Wasn't that the usual procedure?

So he took off his shirt, picked up his wooden Ikea pencil and, there in the darkness, began writing on the fabric the story that was being born in his mind.

CHAPTER ONE

He did not understand why it was forbidden to travel on an aeroplane with a fork when it was perfectly possible to kill someone with a pen. He did not understand why it was forbidden to travel with a knife in one's hand luggage when all the passengers in business class were given one – a metal one, too – so they could eat their in-flight meals with distinction. In fact, he did not understand any of these security measures when it was so easy to kill someone with one's bare hands. If this logic were pursued, shouldn't everyone have their hands – those dangerous weapons – amputated before boarding the plane? Either that, or they should be made to travel in the plane's baggage hold, like the animals, a safe distance from the cockpit.

(Like this dog who is listening to this story right now, and whose glistening eyes are my only landmarks in this blackness? *God Takes a Taxi* will recount the tribulations of a young, blind suicide bomber, an Afghan terrorist by the name of Walid Nadjib, a few minutes before boarding an aeroplane to England. Why blind? Perhaps because I am in darkness at the moment. You only write what you know, after all. The scene will take place in Colombo Airport, in Sri Lanka. But, anyway, back to the story . . .)

The man felt increasingly nervous, repeatedly postponing his passage through the metal detector that separated him from the secure area by locking himself in the toilets. Hidden in the empty tube of his white cane were enough explosives to blow up the aeroplane on which he was about to travel. Nobody suspected blind people.

His plan was foolproof, but the man was now assailed by an unconquerable fear. It was not fear of death, because he was so convinced of the righteousness of his cause that it would be an honour to die in its defence. What worried him was the thought of being arrested before he was able to carry out his plan.

But he had thought of everything. He had spent six months fine-tuning every detail of his last journey. He had managed to get hold of a high-quality fake Sri Lankan passport and a real fake short-stay British business visa. He was wearing a grey, tailor-made suit and carrying a briefcase in which he kept the documents relating to his fictitious company, a car-paint firm that he was going to present to the car manufacturer Vauxhall. He was also carrying samples of the latest colours offered by his company, including puma red and tortoise blue. A myriad of colour tones . . . carried by a blind man! But he had learned his role by heart, so he would be able to answer any question they asked him. He had done everything in his power. The rest was up to the will of Allah.

Without removing his black glasses, the man splashed a little water on his face. Had he not been blind, he would have seen in the bathroom mirror an elegant, clean-shaven old man. Nothing about him suggested he was about blow up an aeroplane somewhere over the Arabian Sea, just after take-off.

After feeling around on the wall, Walid Nadjib pulled a few paper towels from a large metal box and used them to dry his hands. Then, walking without hesitation, he made his way to security. He knew the route by heart. His cane had swept through every square inch. He had walked this way dozens of times, accompanied at first and then alone. Finally, he reached one of the two queues that led to the metal detectors, bumping into the person waiting in line in front of him, and then apologising. He removed his belt. An airport employee came to his aid and helped him with the rest: his suit jacket and his briefcase.

A few seconds later, it was his turn to pass through the metal detector.

(All right, so I've made a start. Now to keep going. The dog barks three times to let me know that's what he's waiting for.)

CHAPTER TWO

The story now moved to a small Sri Lankan prison. Our blind terrorist had been arrested, and this was where he had ended up, without any kind of trial. He had not been sentenced to death, but a prison sentence in this hellhole amounted to the same thing.

Walid Nadjib had been provided with a *bhikkhu* that must once have been red but, after being washed so many times, had now faded to a Guantánamo orange.

The Afghan learned that it was the gown worn by monks in this country, and that it was given to prisoners in the hope that it would purify their souls. Anyway, it didn't matter to him if the gown was a washed-out red because he would never see it.

In his welcome package, there was also a rough bath towel, a packet of ten little bars of soap (it was not advisable to attempt to pick up the soap if you ever dropped it in the shower) and a plastic comb.

So, that day, the man found himself in a

twenty-square-foot cell. As he was old and blind, he was put with just one other prisoner. The other tenants slept four or even five to a room. There was not enough space for everyone here.

His cell mate was called Devanampiya.

'Like Devanampiya Tissa, the Sinhalese king, founder of Anuradhapura. Pleased to meet you, foreigner.'

The Sri Lankan held out his hand to the new arrival in a friendly fashion, but the man did not react. Then, noticing the man's dark glasses, Devanampiya realised that he was blind.

The Afghan spoke a bit of Sinhala, that language in which the tongue strikes hard on the palate and emits little snapping and clicking noises. This helped with the first conversations. Afterwards, Devanampiya decided to teach the blind man his language. They had time. And soon, they were able to have deep discussions about the world, God and the need to make God's voice heard in the world.

The Sri Lankan, even if he was not in agreement with his companion's more radical thinkings, did agree that people should be guided by faith and religion, and that the lack of spirituality in the West could only cause damage to the overall balance of things on Earth. There was no religion on other planets, and the results of that could be easily seen: no life beyond this planet. It just went to show.

One morning, as they were coming out of the showers, the blind man asked Devanampiya if there was a window in their cell. The Sri Lankan thought his cell mate was going to share an escape plan with him.

'I often hear sounds from the town – car engines and bicycle bells – and I smell the scent of sweet peppers on the market. You, who are lucky enough to have eyes and to see the world as it truly is, could you describe to me what you see through that window? That would be so soothing for me.'

Each morning, from that day on, Devanampiya would tell the blind man what was happening outside. He explained that the window had three thick bars, but that there was enough space between them to see the marketplace in front of the prison. In the middle of the square, there were stalls, covered by tarpaulin on rainy days or hot and sunny days. The merchants spread out their brightly coloured food on large wooden trays. These stalls were constantly surrounded by a swarm of customers, and the atmosphere was so effervescent that it was easy to forget that, a few yards away, behind thick stone walls, life had simply stopped for a hundred or so prisoners.

On the left-hand side of the square there was a large house, probably belonging to some rich man. If you stood on tiptoes, you could see the edge of a swimming pool, where sometimes a lady of European origin, her skin dazzlingly white, would swim, wearing very little. But she would disappear almost immediately behind tall trees that had undoubtedly been planted there in order to preserve the inhabitants' privacy and tease the prisoners' imagination.

On the right-hand side, there was a train station, from where you could often hear the metallic screech of the trains' brakes on the rails.

Between the prison and the market, there was a wide street, where all kinds of vehicles circulated. Carts pulled by cattle, modern cars, rickshaws, lorries filled with merchandise, and buses packed with people – hanging from windows, lying on roofs, piled up on running boards. There were bicycles – lots of bicycles, with two or even three people on them – and very old mopeds from England. And, everywhere you looked, people, people, yet more people, as far as the eye could see.

With a vocabulary that was impressively diverse for someone in his position, the Sri Lankan would describe, square inch by square inch, what he saw between the bars. When Walid asked him to explain a word, he would stop his story for a few minutes to become a teacher.

The Afghan remembered everything.

Each day, he would ask for news of the European lady.

'Isn't she swimming today?'

'No. I haven't seen her for several days.'

'And the third merchant from the right, the fat man whose ears are so big you can see them from here, has he sold out of pancakes?'

'Yes. His wife, who has long plaited hair, is cooking more in a frying pan on a camping stove. She needs to be careful she doesn't set fire to her hair!'

'I can smell it from here (the odour of pancakes,

not of burning hair). Mmm . . . that makes me want to take a bite.'

Then the blind man would take a deep breath of the foul potato gruel that he had been served, imagining that it was the long-haired lady's sweet pepper pancakes.

That was how the two men spent their days. Walid became fluent in Sinhala, and Devanampiya was happy to reveal the view, and the life outside, to the blind eyes of his cell mate.

In this way, a great friendship was born between the two men.

Devanampiya's precise, sparkling descriptions punctuated the lonely hours of life in prison. And on days when it rained, and the market was covered with coloured tarpaulins, obstructing the view, or on Tuesdays, when there was no market, the blind man still encouraged his cell mate to describe the scene for him in as much detail as possible.

One day the Sri Lankan, raising himself up on tiptoes by holding tightly to the bars of the window, told Walid about a strange event that had just occurred outside.

'A man in his forties, with a moustache, wearing a white shirt and beige trousers, and walking on crutches, was crossing the street (which was crazy, considering how much traffic there is!) when an old-fashioned yellow car – a sort of New York taxi – sped towards him. Seeing that the car was not going to be able to stop, the young cripple threw away his crutches and ran to the pavement on the other side, where the prison was, without being hit by the car. It was unbelievable!'

'God takes a taxi!' exclaimed Walid, who had been forbidden to call out the name of Allah. 'It's a miracle! So tell me what's happening now . . .'

'I can see a crowd of people, but because it's on our side of the street, it's difficult to see much. My view is blocked by the guard tower. Anyway, there's a huge commotion going on down there. Even the guards have come out into the street.'

'Good, good,' the blind man whispered.
Nothing else of interest happened that day.

CHAPTER THREE

The concept of hygiene in the prison was almost non-existent. Even the water that came out of the shower head was rather dark and muddy. There were cockroaches in the cells, and the prisoners coughed all day and all night. A pestilential stench pervaded the corridors and common areas. The toilets were constantly blocked, and on the rare occasions they became unblocked, gallons of yellowish water overflowed the bowls and flooded onto the broken tiles. When that happened, the prisoners had to paddle in their own excrement, either barefoot or in sandals, like caged animals.

One day, when the two men came back from the patio, where they were allowed to stretch their legs for a few hours each day, Devanampiya – who had been coughing constantly for several weeks – collapsed into the arms of the shocked Walid.

The doctor was called immediately. When he arrived, he examined the young Sri Lankan's body where it lay on the floor. Then he lifted up his stethoscope, shook his head sadly, and two big men dragged the corpse away through the yellowish water in the corridor.

Walid was worried. He asked a passing prisoner

what was happening, and learned that his friend
was dead.

(I wonder if blind people weep. I'll have to check.
If they do, then Walid will cry. He will cry a lot.
The dog barked three times as I was thinking this,
impatient for me to resume my story.)

So Walid wept. (To be checked.)
He cried his eyes out that night. He was heart-
broken. His sobs could be heard as far away as his
home, in Afghanistan. He had lost a friend, his only
friend, and with Devanampiya, he had also lost his
ability to see. Under these circumstances, prison
would soon become a hell again.

CHAPTER FOUR

Walid Nadjib did not have time to get used to
being alone in his cell. A few days later, there was
a knock, and the thick wooden door creaked on
its hinges.

'We would have left you alone,' said the guard, 'but there's no more space. I hope this will be all right.'

He had spoken the last sentence as if he knew something about the new arrival that the blind man didn't; something that did not bode well.

The door banged shut again, and a deathly silence rose to fill the room. The Afghan spoke first, as if to exorcise an evil spell. He introduced himself, not forgetting to tell his new cell mate that he was blind and that he would appreciate it if the new arrival would speak to him.

But the new arrival did not say a thing.

The straw in one of the beds crunched like salad leaves being slowly chewed. The new arrival must have lain down. Soon he was asleep and breathing so loudly, like a snoring bear, that Walid's ears hurt. The blind man thought his new companion must be very tired, so he didn't disturb him.

A few hours later, at mealtime, the man woke up and ate his gruel. Walid could hear him chewing and belching; it was as if he were inside the man's stomach. As the man was awake, Walid spoke to him.

'I apologise if I said something to offend you

earlier. I am blind and I cannot see the expression on your face. If you don't speak to me, I am afraid I will never know with whom I am sharing these sad walls. The time will pass much more quickly if we trust each other. Well, that's what I think, anyway . . .'

The other man did not reply.

Walid continued to hear the man munching his gruel. It sounded like boots stomping through mud. Intrigued, he stood up and groped his way forward until his hands touched his cell mate's clammy skin. The man stopped chewing.

'Stop feeling me up, you old perv!' shouted the man in a version of Sinhala seriously mangled by elocution problems. 'I've killed men for less than that!'

Walid removed his hand instantly, as if he'd touched fire.

'No, no, don't get me wrong! I'm blind. I just wanted to get your attention because you hadn't spoken a word to me since your arri—'

'There's no point wasting your breath,' the Sri Lankan interrupted in a stammer. 'I'm deaf as a post.'

The news fell like the blade of a guillotine.

The new arrival was an imposing man, six-foot-six tall with big muscles and a fat belly. A thin black moustache covered his top lip, as if to say 'not one word will escape this mouth'. But Targuyn, thanks to laborious articulation exercises, had managed to learn speech, in spite of the pessimistic predictions of all the doctors who had examined him. So Targuyn was no longer mute, only deaf, a handicap he could do nothing to alter.

As soon as he had entered the cell, he had been struck by the strangeness of this man in sunglasses. What was the point of wearing something like that in a place where the sunlight barely penetrated?

With his dark glasses and his wandering hands, the prisoner definitely seemed like a pervert. He had probably been locked in this miserable place, deprived of any sexual outlet, for several years – long enough, anyway, to warp his judgement, so that when he looked at a moustachioed giant weighing twenty-eight stone, he saw a desirable twenty-year-old virgin.

And then suddenly it all became clear. The dark glasses, the way the man moved through the cell groping with his hands, the white cane leaning against the walls. All these clues finally indicated to Targuyn, who was a bit slow on the uptake, that his cell mate was blind.

One of us deaf and the other blind, he thought. What a joke!

As night was falling, Targuyn got up from his bed and approached the blind man, who was sitting with his face to the ceiling, his lips quivering. He looked like he was either going crazy or praying.

'My name is Targuyn,' he said simply.

So Walid discovered that the giant was not a bad man, after all.

(What can happen next? Quick, I need an idea! The dog is barking.)

The two men soon became friends, because each of them had something that differentiated him from everyone else. The first could not see, and the second could not hear. In some ways, they completed one another. What one could not see, the other could describe for him. What one could not hear, the other could write for him.

Targuyn had never seen a blind man write before. With one hand, Walid touched the edge of the paper, so he wouldn't go beyond it, and with the other he wrote in letters that were as tiny as possible. The lines he wrote went off in every direction, forming pretty pile-ups of words.

Walid, who missed Devanampiya a little more every day and thought of him nostalgically, one day repeated to Targuyn the strange request he had once made to his former cell mate.

He wrote: 'Deskryb for me wot you sea threw that windoe.'

So many questions had been buzzing around Walid's head since his friend's death. What Targuyn had taken for prayers, quivering on Walid's lips as he sat in a delirium, had actually been a recital of Devanampiya's descriptions, remembered by the blind man and repeated to himself as a way of restoring the blessed illusion of sight that had marked the first months of his incarceration.

And so, on the first day of spring, the giant read the words Walid had scratched with a pen on a scrap of paper. While it was true that he spoke Sinhala fluently, the Afghan struggled badly with his spellings.

'You write better than some native speakers, Walid. There are a few mistakes, but I can still get the gist. On the other hand, I don't really understand what you want. Tell me, and I will grant your wish.'

Targuyn sometimes spoke like the genies who come out of lamps in fairy tales. But the blind man's only response was to tap the piece of paper with his finger, insisting upon what he had written.

'The window looks out on a wall,' said the giant. 'A brick wall. There's nothing to see.'

For a moment, the blind man did not react.

'What?'

Walid looked as though he had been turned into a stone statue.

Then, slowly, he bowed his head.

His world had collapsed.

He understood that his former cell mate had invented all those descriptions just to make him happy. A generous, selfless gesture. A gesture of love, fraternity, friendship.

(All right, so I've covered the front of the shirt with writing, and both sleeves, and now I have just finished the back. Unless I'm mistaken, there is no space left. And anyway, I don't know what to write next. I need to revise it, but I think it's pretty good for a first novel . . .)

The pride he felt at having put his ideas into words was the third electric shock that the fakir received to his heart during this adventure. He knew this was a good story, and that all he had to do was write it on paper and it would become a book. He promised himself he would do that as soon as he arrived at his destination, wherever that might be. After first telephoning Marie, of course. That couldn't wait.

Italy

'And that is how I ended up inside your trunk, madame,' Ajatashatru concluded with a half-smile.

Disappearing inside a piece of luggage in Barcelona and reappearing in Rome was, by far, the best magic trick he had ever performed. Houdini could not have done better.

The beautiful young woman with green eyes and brown hair looked at him, her expression wavering between surprise, scepticism and the desire to scream. But this was better than the hysterics that had gripped her when she had first opened the trunk and discovered him. She lowered the bedside lamp she had picked up as a weapon. The story was far-fetched, admittedly, but there was something sincere and genuine in the man's tone. And how could anyone come up with such a ridiculous lie?

'I will now leave this room. I will not bother you any more, madame. I will vanish completely from your life. But before I do, I would like to ask you a question.'

'All right, I'm listening,' she managed to stammer in excellent English.

'Where are we? This must be the fourth time I've wondered that in the last two days. You can't imagine how annoying that is . . .'

'In Rome,' replied Sophie Morceaux. 'At the Hotel Parco dei Principi.'

'Ah. You mean Rome in Italy?'

'Yes, yes. Rome in Italy,' confirmed the Bond girl from *Tomorrow Is Not Enough*. 'Do you know another one?'

'No.'

The man seemed so harmless and the situation so comical that the actress could not help smiling. Having thought at first that he was some kind of maniacal fan, she now felt relieved.

She looked at this Indian, tall, thin and gnarled like a tree, with a large moustache. His white, crumpled shirt was covered with tiny writing. It looked like a shroud printed with pencilled hieroglyphics.

'What is that?' she asked, pointing to his shirt.

'That? Pencil. An Ikea pencil, in fact. But, to be

more precise, my latest novel . . . or rather, my first novel, written in the dark.'

'Do you usually write your books on your shirts?'

'Would you rather I'd written it on yours?' joked Ajatashatru.

Sophie Morceaux giggled. Then she turned towards her open and hopelessly empty trunk.

'Talking of my clothes, I presume they must have stayed in Barcelona. In fact, if I understand you correctly, I have nothing else to wear.'

Ajatashatru bowed his head like a guilty child. He did not have the courage to tell her that he had kept a pair of her knickers in his trouser pocket.

'Me neither,' he said.

Little remained of the beautiful suit, shirt and tie that he had rented from old Dilawar. The jacket and the tie were mouldering in France, and the shirt was covered with the opening pages of a novel.

'Well, I didn't like those dresses anyway,' Sophie Morceaux lied. 'This is Gucci and Versace country, after all,' she added, happy at the idea of going on a shopping spree. 'It shouldn't be too difficult to find something, should it?'

'I think . . .' said Ajatashatru, who never knew how to reply to negative questions.

'So, do you have any plans for the evening? What time does your next wardrobe leave?'

For the first time in his life, someone was trusting him, just like that, without him having to come up with a cheap trick or clever ploy, but simply by him telling the truth. The 'good countries' really were a box of chocolates full of surprises. And the welcoming committee was not always composed of policemen. His homesickness lifted for a few seconds.

This was the fourth electric shock that the fakir received to his heart during this adventure. He had been helped again. But when would he be able to help someone else?

Moved by the Indian's story, Sophie Morceaux had asked him to spend the evening with her. He was a mysterious, original and sincere character, and his presence allowed her to forget, for the time it took them to eat dinner, the watered-down, super-ficial personalities with whom she had been rubbing shoulders ever since she began starring in American blockbusters. Moreover, she did not entirely believe his story and preferred to imagine that Ajatashatru was a political writer, in hiding from the authorities in his country, who had been forced to travel il-legally in order to reach Europe and seek asylum. Yes, that was much more exciting.

The hotel where the actress was staying for the next few days, in order to attend the Festival of Latin Cinema, was situated on a hillside in the Italian capital, just behind the beautiful Villa Borghese gardens, a breathing space in this frantic city.

As the Parco dei Principi Grand Hotel & Spa was much too expensive for *A-jar-of-rat-stew*, the correct pronunciation of his name, which she managed to say perfectly, she had invited him to sleep in the room next to hers, room 605, which her manager had reserved, along with a dozen other rooms on the same floor, so that the star would not be disturbed by her fans.

It really was worth travelling in a trunk if you were then given a night in a room in one of the most luxurious hotels in Rome, separated only by a dividing wall from the most beautiful woman in the world. The Indian did feel a little guilty, however. Assefa and his friends were probably not so well off at this very moment. He imagined them sitting in the back of a freight truck crossing the Franco-Spanish border, eating tinned food and chocolate biscuits while they waited for the police to arrest them again.

While he had no idea what was going to happen to him from one minute to the next, the Indian was happy to be where he was. He ought to have been in the aeroplane, on his way home. But, strange as it may seem, he didn't wish that were the case. Here and now, at least, the pressure was off for a moment.

He reminded himself that he was in the middle of an incredible journey and that he was meeting some wonderful people. And he had to make the most of this euphoric mood because, very soon, he would probably be moping about in his bed, alone, prey to the most intense form of depression – that felt by exiles, people torn from their roots, homebodies who find themselves miles from the places they know and love, who are so homesick they can feel it in their veins, as if they are floating down a river without a single branch to hold onto.

He thought of his cousin Parthasarathy, so far away. He would have liked so much to be able to share all these emotional moments, but perhaps if he had been here, none of this would have happened. The two of them would certainly never have fitted inside the Vuitton trunk. Never mind – he would tell his cousin all about it when he got home, if he ever did get home. If only he had been able to keep his family up to date on his progress as it happened. In two days in Europe, he had seen things he had never seen in thirty-eight years of existence, things he would undoubtedly never have seen if he had not one day decided to hide inside a wardrobe in a large furniture store. It just went to show how tenuous life was, and how the most ordinary places could sometimes be the start of the most exciting adventures.

Once he was inside his deluxe room, Ajatashatru jumped onto the double bed to test its comfort. My life as a bohemian and charlatan is over, he thought. I have other ambitions now. Including, in no particular order, helping someone, publishing my book and seeing Marie again.

Satisfied with the mattress, he got off the bed and went to the bathroom. There was a white claw-foot bathtub with gold taps. The Indian thought that a nice hot bath would be the right way to begin a new life. It would be like washing all his sins away.

When he re-emerged from the bathroom one hour later, in a soft, white dressing gown, he found clean clothes folded neatly on his bed. A beautiful brown shirt, beige jacket and trousers, ecru socks and cream shoes. There were more shades of beige here than on a Pantone colour chart. A note on headed paper, left on the bedside table and written in a pretty feminine hand, informed him: *I will see you in one hour in the lobby.*

He quickly put on the clothes. They all fitted him perfectly, as if they had been made to measure. He was not exactly a fashion connoisseur, true, but the sleeves were neither too long nor too short, and the hems of his trousers fell neatly onto his shoes.

Ajatashatru admired himself in the room's large smoked-glass mirror. He did not recognise himself. He looked fantastic. Now, he really did look like a wealthy Indian industrialist. What elegance! He could hardly believe the man in the mirror was actually him. He thought he looked very handsome. If he'd had a camera, he would have taken a picture and sent it to Marie. But he did not have a camera, nor did he have her address. And anyway, this suit was just a facade. He did not have everything that went with it. The watch, the computer, the mobile phone, the car, the house, the Swiss bank account. Why was Sophie being so generous to him? He was a stranger. And he still hadn't had the opportunity to help anyone. He wondered what it would look like, the face of the first person he would help.

For now, the only face he saw was his own. He took a step towards the mirror. There was something missing from this idyllic picture, something that would make the transformation complete. Or, rather, there was something that ought to be missing.

For the first time in his life, the Indian removed the piercings from his ears and his fleshy lips and shaved his moustache, taking as much care as if this were his last day on Earth. This was, in fact, the final act in his metamorphosis and disappearance. The fakir had evaporated forever in the steamy bathroom, and a writer had been born.

During the half-hour that remained before he had to meet Sophie, Ajatashatru decided to telephone Marie, as he had promised himself he would if he survived his journey in the baggage hold of the aeroplane. He regretted not having a mobile phone, like his cousin Parthasarathy. The official reason was that a telepath did not need one; the unofficial reason was that he didn't have enough money; the real, shameful reason was that he had no one to call. So, he made do with the landline at his adoptive mother's house.

He telephoned the hotel reception and asked to be put through to the number the Frenchwoman had scribbled on the chewing-gum wrapper.

While the telephone rang, the Indian's heart began pounding in his chest like a techno song. What would he say to her? Did she still remember him? Had she waited for him?

These questions remained unanswered, because

no one picked up the phone. Simultaneously disappointed and relieved, he hung up, and his Coca-Cola eyes were sad. He wanted to see Marie again. He was sure of that now. What on earth had made him reject her advances? He had not wanted to get involved for fear it would compromise his mission. But what was that great mission? Buying a bed of nails that would be no use to him whatsoever now that he was a writer? Although it could be used to make shelves when it was disassembled, he supposed. Fifteen thousand nails – that would have been hours of fun for all the family! But, anyway, he had not bought that useless bed of nails. So much the better.

How stupid he had been! He thought again about the porcelain doll's hand when it had gently touched his. He had pushed it away. Never would he have such an opportunity again. He walked slowly to the bathroom, and picked up his old shirt from the edge of the bidet, where he had left it while he had a bath. Then he went into the bedroom and sat down at the desk.

He took one of the hotel's pens and a large sheet of paper and began to meticulously copy out what he had written in the baggage hold. At times the shirt was difficult to read. It had not been easy, writing in the dark. Like his blind protagonist, he had used one finger to guide his pencil so that he was not writing on nothing. The letters were tiny and some of them had been rubbed out in places, transforming his novel into an exercise in filling in the blanks. But as he was the author, it was not too difficult for him to remember his words or to invent others.

He wondered what had become of his first listener – the dog in the baggage hold. As he had climbed back inside his hiding place when the aeroplane landed, Ajatashatru had never actually seen the face – or, rather, the muzzle – of his travelling companion. The animal could never have imagined that it had witnessed the last hours of the fakir Ajatashatru and the first hours of Ajatashatru the writer. It had enjoyed a ringside seat for the greatest human transformation ever to take place in the hold of an aeroplane.

The Rajasthani looked at the window. Outside, the sun was disappearing behind the trees in the garden. Time had passed quickly. He put down his pen and stood up. He would finish this later. Above all, he did not want to be late for his first ever date.

As soon as Gustave Palourde saw the luxury clothes thrown on the floor, next to the baggage carousel, he realised that the man he was looking for must have emptied out a suitcase in order to hide inside it. At that moment, the Hindu must be somewhere on the runway, ready to be loaded into the hold of an aeroplane heading to Italy.

The gypsy might have told the other gypsy, Tom Cruise-Jesús, to drive him to the aeroplane. There, he could have inspected the baggage holds and stabbed his ivory-handled Opinel knife through every bag that might possibly have contained the tall, thin and tree-like body of his sworn enemy.

But he didn't do that. He had a much better idea.

Not all the holds were pressurised and heated; that depended on the model of the plane. So there was a good chance that, during the flight, the Indian would be transformed into a very large ice cube. The baggage handler confirmed that, at 36,000 feet, which was the cruising altitude of a commercial flight, the temperature would be minus 56.5 degrees Celsius. Which explains why suitcases are often cold when you pick them up from the baggage carousel.

If the hold was not pressurised, there was even less to worry about. The thief's head would explode inside his turban soon after take-off.

Nevertheless, Gustave was a far-sighted guy. In the eventuality that the thief survived (some particularly determined illegal aliens from Africa and South America had been found, frozen but alive, hidden in the undercarriages of planes), he would prepare a special welcoming committee in Rome. Gustave's cousin Gino, a hairdresser by profession, had been living in the Italian capital for a few years now.

But first he had to find out exactly where it was going, the suitcase in which the Indian was hiding, because Rome was a vast playing field. He decided it would be wise to delegate this investigation to the perfect ally: his wife. Because, as the young Spanish baggage handler had so brilliantly deduced, the clothes that had been thrown away appeared to belong to someone rich, or important, or both. And Gustave's wife, as a shrewd and devoted reader of all the tabloid magazines, knew all the rich, or important, or both, people on planet Earth. In less time than it took to say it in sign language, she would lead him to the clothes' owner like Professor Calculus's clock had led Tintin to the seven crystal balls.

The taxi driver was not disappointed when he took a few samples from the pile of clothing to Mercedes-Shayana, who was sitting on the terrace of the airport bar with their daughter.

'Mother of God!' she cried out, after inspecting a black dress set with diamonds. 'That looks like Sophie Morceaux's dress!'

The woman had recognised the low-cut ball gown, which the famous actress had worn when she climbed the steps at the Cannes Film Festival last May.

Mercedes-Shayana measured the garment with her thumb and then, with both hands, held the fabric close to her face like a professional dressmaker examining her latest work. Yes, it was the right size. And after her husband had explained to her where he had found these fabulous clothes, she gave him a confident, satisfied look and announced that there was a very good chance that the clothes really did belong to the film star. In fact, she was so confident of this fact that she swore to it on the life of her daughter, who was at that moment flirting with the young baggage handler.

'These clothes belong to Sophie Morceaux. I would swear it on the life of my daughter WHO IS FLIRTING WITH THE BAGGAGE HANDLER! Ssshhh!'

While making shooing noises, the woman waved her hand in the air as if to scare away flies, or possibly young people flirting in front of their mother.

'Very good, very good,' said Gustave, stroking his gold-bedecked fingers. 'Now, Tom Cruise-Jesús, it's up to you.'

'Sorry?' said the young Spaniard distractedly, upon hearing his name.

Since he worked in the airport, it would not be too difficult for the young man to check whether the French actress was on the passenger list for the Rome-Fiumicino flight. And if she was, it would not be too difficult to discover which taxi company her manager had booked for her arrival. Then, he could find out where the star was staying during her time in Rome, and his mission would be complete.

'Do you understand?' asked Gustave, removing

the hand of the handsome *hidalgo* from that of his daughter. 'If you bring me all this information, you will have a reward,' he added, nodding to Miranda-Jessica.

'It shouldn't be a problem,' said the happy, highly motivated young man.

'Very good, very good. When you know a bit more, you should come and eat dinner with us. We have a little seaside apartment in Barceloneta.'

With these words, the gypsy picked up his wife's beer mat and wrote an address on it.

'*Hasta luego.*'

The women stood and Gustave picked up his ice cooler.

'Can I keep all these, Gus?' asked Mercedes-Shayana, pointing at the pile of clothes.

'They're yours, my love,' replied the taxi driver, already imagining his wife in Sophie Morceaux's fine lingerie.

'You're a doll, Gus. You'll see how good your little wife looks . . .'

She put on one of the dresses, a sort of pink Roman toga, over her flowery dressing gown. It matched the colour of her leggings and sandals, after all. Classy! she thought.

Mercedes-Shayana could already see herself on the beach, strutting barefoot in the sand, wearing her new clothes.

As for her daughter, Miranda-Jessica was already working out how she could steal the sexy outfits from her mother in order to seduce the young Spanish baggage handler. She had forgotten all about Kevin-Jésus.

Meanwhile, Gustave was imagining piercing the Indian like a pie crust that you don't want to puff up.

And Tom Cruise-Jesús was thinking that he had better live up to his first first name in this Mission Impossible if he wanted to win the pretty blonde.

Sophie Morceaux had not had any trouble finding a new evening dress. So she appeared in the hotel lobby for her date wearing a grey bustier dress, her brown hair decorated by a discreet diamond-encrusted diadem.

Ajatashatru, who had already become used to the luxury of the palatial hotel and who was at that moment busy decoding an Italian newspaper, lifted his Coca-Cola eyes to the young woman. They sparkled like the drink does when it is poured into a glass.

'You look radiant!'

'Thank you. You're not too bad yourself like that. You look younger without your moustache. You ought to wash your turban, though – it's a little dirty.'

'I never take off my turban,' said the Indian, sounding faintly offended.

But he did think that perhaps he should wash it

before he saw Marie again. You never knew: perhaps all Frenchwomen thought the same way? And he did not want to make a bad impression on the woman who made his heart pound like a Bollywood soundtrack.

At that moment, a somewhat portly European man, dressed in loose white linen clothes that gave him an improbable look – something between the guru of a sect and an ambulance driver – entered the lobby and moved towards Sophie Morceaux.

'Come on, Sophie, we'll be late,' he said in a language that the Rajasthani did not understand, but which he identified nonetheless as being French.

'Hervé, let me introduce you to my friend Ajatashatru Oghash. Ajatashatru, this is Hervé, my manager.'

The Indian nodded and shook the man's hand, which was big, fat, soft and clammy.

'*A-Japanese-ass-toot?*' repeated the plump Frenchman, wondering what kind of awful parents could have given such a name to their child. 'Nice talking to you.'

Then he took his young protégée by the arm and led her towards the exit without paying any further attention to the Indian.

'Ajatashatru is coming with us!' protested the actress, when she realised that her manager had not included the Indian in his plans.

'Sophie, this is an important dinner. We have to get you that role in the next Beccassini film.'

'By *we*, what you actually mean is *I*,' Sophie corrected him.

If her eyes had been lasers, the French manager's pounds of fat would have melted away more quickly than they would on a Weight Watchers diet.

The Hindu, whose knowledge of French was limited to the few words he heard on Indian television at Christmas – namely, *eau de toilette pour l'homme, eau de toilette pour la femme*, and *le nouveau parfum de Christian Dior* – did not need a dictionary to understand that he was the centre of a quarrel between his protector and her manager. Embarrassed by this, he caught up with them and said in English:

'Don't worry about me. I'll stay in the hotel this evening. Anyway, I do have an excuse. I'm exhausted after travelling in the trunk. And I didn't sleep at all last night.'

Hervé, who spoke a little bit of the language of Shakespeare, did not know what the man meant by *travelling in the trunk.* He assumed it must be an English expression, but it didn't bode well as far as he was concerned, particularly coming from a guy named *A-Japanese-ass-toot*. He took Sophie aside and asked her who this Indian was and where he had come from. To the first question, the actress replied that her friend was Rajasthani and that he was a brilliant writer who had been persecuted in his own country. To the second, that he had come from her Vuitton trunk, but that Hervé should just drop the subject because he wouldn't understand.

So the manager had to resign himself to the fact that Sophie's new friend was coming with them. It was either that or having her storm up to her hotel room and thus miss out on the irresistible contract that they were going to be offered. He knew from experience that there was no point arguing with temperamental stars once they got an idea in their head.

And so, around 8.30 p.m., the taxi dropped them off in front of an impressive stone building covered by a gigantic ivy plant and thousands of flowers. A white-and-red sign on the wall said *Il Gondoliere*. It was evidently an Italian restaurant, but that was hardly surprising as they were in Italy.

Hervé gave the name of Emilie Jolie to the maître d', who nodded as if this were a secret code known only to initiates and led them to a very good table at the back of the restaurant, tucked away discreetly in a corner.

Five minutes later, two eccentric-looking men arrived at their table. Ajatashatru understood that one of them, the tallest, was the film director Mick Jagger-LeCoultre. He looked like some kind of rock star, and his wrists were covered with watches. The other, who seemed to be his manager, was a small fat man with soft, clammy hands whose name was Steve. The Indian looked from Hervé to Steve, wondering if all managers of stars were cast from the same mould.

'Sophie, it's an honour to meet you,' said the tall rock star, taking the actress's hand and gently kissing it.

His refined manners did not suit his appearance at all. Jeans with holes, piercings, dyed red hair, faded green jacket. He looked like a cross between a fakir and a clown.

When he turned towards the Indian, the Frenchwoman introduced him as her new friend.

'Wonderful,' said the extravagant film director. 'And how did you two meet?'

'Well, I just opened my trunk, and there he was!'
Everyone laughed.

'I don't suppose you were born in a trunk, though,
Mr *I-just-had-sex-too* . . .'

'I come from Rajasthan.'

A wind of admiration blew around the table.

'Very interesting. And what do you do?' asked
Mick Jagger-LeCoultre's manager.

Ajatashatru was tempted to say the word 'fakir',
as he had always done, but this was no longer what
he did.

'I'm a writer.'

'And Ajatashatru is not just any writer,' added
Sophie Morceaux. 'He writes his novels on his
shirts.'

'Oh, really? How original!' exclaimed the film
director, who liked people as extravagant as himself.
'And are your shirts published?'

The Indian smiled. 'To be honest, I'm just getting
started.'

'But that's wonderful! Let's raise our glasses to
the birth of a great career.'

Everyone lifted their glass of champagne,
Ajatashatru his glass of water.

'Do you have a publisher?'

'Um . . . no.'

'We might be able to arrange that. Don't you think, Hervé?' Sophie said, batting her eyelids at her manager.

Although initially reticent about the idea, the man thought for a moment, then agreed, as he always did, to grant his protégée's wish.

'All right, all right, I know someone at Éditions d'Havoc.' He turned to the Indian and said, 'Give me your manuscript tomorrow morning and I'll get it to him.'

'Fantastic!' cried Sophie, jumping from her chair like a little girl who has been given exactly what she wants.

The rest of the meal passed uneventfully, apart from the signing of the major contract. Chocolate profiteroles for some, tiramisu for others, more champagne, more water for the brand-new author.

So that, to cut a long story short, was how Ajatashatru Oghash Rathod, commonly known as 'Oh gosh!', fakir turned writer, dipped his toe into the inviting waters of his new celebrity life and witnessed the signing of one of the biggest movie contracts in history. And as no one ever changes completely, and as it is difficult to erase in a few seconds a whole life spent performing magic tricks, our Indian gave in to temptation, between dessert and coffee, bending a spoon just by looking at it and then stabbing a toothpick into his eye, to the amusement and horror of the other diners.

Nestled in his sumptuous linen sheets, Ajatashatru was now crying like a baby. Here it was at last, the depression he had been dreading. Well, it had to hit him at some point. He had become entangled in an uncertain journey, with no end in sight, far from his home and loved ones, and – as if that were not enough – a vindictive killer was following him around, reappearing every time the situation started to improve.

It was too much pressure for one poor fakir to bear.

He looked up to the ceiling. A ray of light was shining in above the curtains, illuminating the opposite wall, on which hung a gold-framed painting by Jesus Capilla. The picture showed a countryside landscape. Two peasants, wearing nineteenth-century clothing, were standing, apparently in silent contemplation, in front of a hay bale.

The Indian envied the two old men their

tranquillity. He found their company soothing. Despite the anachronism, he would have liked to stand next to them, motionless and silent. To spend his whole life looking at that hay bale and to never know this pain that gets you in the stomach. He knew that the gypsy would never come to look for him there, in that field. And if by any chance he did turn up, his peasant friends would defend him with their big pitchforks.

Ajatashatru wiped his eyes with the bed sheet. A few minutes later, soothed by the painting, his sobbing and his tiredness, he fell gently into the arms of Shiva.

The next morning, around 9.30 a.m., Ajatashatru woke with a start, covered in sweat after a nightmare in which his cousin Parthasarathy, transformed into a cherry tomato, was being roasted on a skewer over a fire. Around him, happy gypsies played guitar and danced. Parthasarathy cried out in pain and nobody cared. Only Ajatashatru seemed to understand the sufferings of his cousin, but as he too was impaled on the same skewer, in the form of pieces of chopped (holy) cow, he was not in a position to do much about it.

The Indian rubbed his eyes. He praised Buddha that he was in a luxurious hotel room in Italy and not on a sharp metal rod about to be crammed down the throats of starving gypsies. He also remembered that he was supposed to have arrived in New Delhi the previous day, and that he had not even told Parthasarathy about the change in plans. His cousin might still be waiting for him at the airport, angry or worried. He had a feeling that, when he did finally go back to India, he would end up smeared with olive oil and garlic on that skewer he had seen in his dream, but that his fellow countrymen would be the ones dancing around the fire. This idea did not enchant the writer, despite his self-torturing past as a fakir.

So Ajatashatru called down to reception and asked them to ring Adishree's home number, the only telephone number he knew, apart from Marie's. His cousin had changed mobile phones so often that Ajatashatru had never felt the need to learn all the different numbers by heart.

The telephone rang a few times, and then an old lady's voice echoed in the receiver. She burst into sobs when she realised it was her little Aja calling. She had been so worried. What had happened to him?

'Yesterday, your . . . cousin was waiting . . . for you all night,' she stammered through her tears. 'He moved heaven . . . and Earth to find out . . . what had happened to you. At the airport, they consulted the passenger list for your flight . . . they told him you didn't catch the aeroplane. Why did you . . . stay in Paris, my boy? Are you all right?'

She had always talked to him as if he were a little boy, her little boy. It was her way of dealing with the fact that she had never been able to have children of her own.

'I'm not in Paris any more, dear Adishree. I'm in Rome.'

'Rome?' the old lady shouted, her tears suddenly stopping.

'It's a long story. Tell Parthasarathy that I'm fine. Tell him I've become an honest man, a writer. I'll come back soon.'

The old lady was disconcerted by these words. An honest man, a writer? What was he talking about? Ajatashatru had always been an honest boy, as far as she knew. Not only that, but ever since childhood he had been blessed with special powers that made him even more extraordinary. For a moment, she thought that he had lost his gift; that would explain this sudden and incongruous change of occupation. Writer? Why not dance the foxtrot or become a jockey?

'Don't worry,' Ajatashatru repeated, unaware that those words just made the old lady worry even more.

After a few more consoling words, he hung up.

Without letting go of the handset, he called the hotel reception again and asked them to try once more with the French number he had vainly attempted to call the previous evening. After a few rings, Marie's marvellous voice echoed in the receiver.

'Marie?'

'Ajatashatru? Is that really you?'

She spoke to him as if he were a close friend.

'Yes, it's me.'

There was silence on the line for a few seconds. So, she remembered him.

'Are you still in Paris?'

'No. I'm in Rome.'

This reply seemed to take Marie by surprise. In her mind, there had been only two places where the Rajasthani was likely to be at that moment – Paris or *Quiche-and-yogurt*, his village in India.

'In Rome?'

'Professional necessities,' said Ajatashatru, as if he had been using this phrase all his life. 'I was calling you to say that . . .'

He hesitated, like a teenager making his first phone call to a girl. The rhythm of his heartbeat went from hip hop to techno, finally ending up on Vivaldi.

'I would like to go back to Paris to see you again.'

Cupid's arrow flew straight into Marie's heart. The man had pronounced each word with a tenderness that made her eyes shine. She blushed, and felt relieved that her face was not visible on the telephone. She felt suddenly younger. 'To see me again,' she repeated. Perhaps this was silly, but it seemed to her that no one had said anything so sweet, so nice to her in years. The youngsters she found on her nights out never wanted to see her again. And they were not as sweet or nice as Ajatashatru either. They were unbridled beasts who wanted her only to calm their juvenile, testosterone-fuelled urges.

'I loved our conversation, our laughter, your eyes,' he continued, his voice still tender. 'I have to finish up a few things in Rome, and then I'm coming. See you soon,' he concluded, feeling embarrassed.

If Marie had learned one thing, it was that you could fall in love at forty years old with a stranger you met in an Ikea cafeteria. It was perhaps not very sensible, but God, it felt good! It just went to show that nothing was ever lost. An Ajatashatru pill was better than all the antidepressants in the world. She replaced the receiver, her heart devoured by the flames of a wildfire.

Ajatashatru hung up. He realised that, when he had called down to reception a few minutes earlier to ask them to put him in contact with France, he had not had the faintest idea what he was going to say to Marie. That he was fine, that he was thinking about her. What else? He would just be keeping the promise he had made to himself in the aeroplane's hold. To call her if he survived. That was all. He was not accustomed to having telephone conversations, least of all with ladies.

But his heart had spoken for him. 'I have to finish up a few things in Rome, and then I'm coming,' he had heard himself say. Where? To Paris? When? And, most pressingly, how? He had no idea. More empty words! More lies!

How could he get to Paris? He was so full of crap. 'I have to finish up a few things in Rome, and then I'm coming,' he had said, as though it were the most natural thing in the world, as though he had enough money to pay for that kind of luxury. His head was full of a rich man's plans, but the truth was he did not even have one Indian rupee in his pocket. All he had was a beautiful, beige designer suit.

He imagined himself sitting at the back of a truck full of potatoes, in his posh suit, feeling that fear in his gut each time the truck slowed down. There had to be another way.

Oh, never mind, I'll think about it later.

He swept these thoughts from his mind, lay down on the bed and put on the sports channel.

In Paris, as we have already said, Marie replaced the receiver, her heart devoured by the flames of a wildfire – a sentence that does not really mean much, but which does, Ajatashatru thought, possess a certain literary flair.

For a few moments, she stared at the wall in silence.

'Everything all right, Marie?'

The woman turned towards the handsome, twenty-five-year-old Adonis whom she had found a few hours earlier in the yogurt aisle of the local supermarket. He was lying on her bed, a cigarette in his mouth, frowning in concentration as he did his version of a post-coital James Dean.

'Go home, Franck.'

'It's Benjamin,' the young man corrected her.

'Go home, Benjamin.'

He must have been used to being kicked out of bed by his female conquests because he got up and dressed without batting an eyelid, the cigarette still in his mouth, still frowning in concentration.

When she was finally alone, Marie tore the sheets from the bed and threw them in the laundry basket. She disgusted herself sometimes. How could she have fallen back into her old routine? Out of solitude, undoubtedly, and the desire to be considered attractive. But those youngsters she snacked on from time to time were mere insects next to Aja. He was a man, a real man. A savage with pierced lips and ears. A moustachioed god with olive skin and Coca-Cola eyes. When I'm with him, I feel like a little girl. Never in my life have I felt as protected as I did in the Ikea restaurant. Maybe I'm holding onto a dead branch. Maybe all of this is just an illusion, a chimera. But why shouldn't I believe, if that's what I want to do? He is different. Perhaps the two of us have more in common than appearances would suggest?

Oh, never mind, I'll think about it later.

She swept these thoughts from her mind, lay down on the bed and put on the sports channel.

At midday, Ajatashatru went down to the lobby. Coming back from the restaurant the previous evening, he had gone up to his room and finished copying out his manuscript so he could give it to Hervé. By now, the Frenchman would have handed it to the publisher, who was staying in Rome this week.

Sophie Morceaux was waiting for him, reading a French book, the title of which Ajatashatru did not understand, as it did not contain the words *eau de toilette, homme, femme, nouveau parfum* or *Christian Dior*. Instead it seemed to say something like *On Winter Mornings the Rabbits Yelp Lugubriously on the Road* by a certain Angélique Dutoit Delamaison. Sensing his presence, the young woman looked up and slid a pretty red bookmark between the pages she had been reading.

'Change of plans, Aja. We'll eat lunch together a

bit later. The editor from Éditions d'Havoc wants
to meet you.'

'Oh. When?'

'Right now,' replied the actress, pointing with her
slender finger to the lobby bar, where Hervé was
drinking a cocktail with another man. 'Tell me all
about it afterwards,' she added with a happy smile.

Sheepishly, the writer walked the few yards that
separated him from the two men. Why did the
publisher want to see him so quickly? Had he even
had time to read the manuscript?'

'The great *I-jab-at-you-to-thank-you*!' announced
Hervé, getting to his feet.

'*Jabba-the-Hutt's-back-tooth*?' said the other
man. 'What a fantastic name!'

'My name is Ajatashatru, but you may call me
Marcel, if that's easier.'

'My name is Gérard François – typical French
name, you know?' said the publisher in perfect
English. 'Not very original compared to yours . . .
Anyway, I read your novel, or rather your short
story, because it's not very long. I heard you wrote
it on your shirt? You should have continued it on
your trousers . . . But, anyway, I liked it a lot.'

The three men sat down. Gérard François did

not look like either of the celebrity managers. In fact, he was the exact opposite. He was not fat and did not have clammy hands. He was a tall man, with an athletic build. He had the blue eyes and handsome, tanned face of a ski instructor. He was wearing an elegant designer suit and a tie, despite the heat. So he looked like a skier and had a name like a French singer: a nice mix.

'One thing about it does bother me, though – the end. Change the end,' he said with the air of a man used to giving orders and seeing them carried out. 'Because I've read that story before, only in a hospital.'

Beautiful people command respect more easily than ugly people, the Indian thought. They exercise a sort of natural attraction. They also arouse the admiration and envy of others. It's a sort of manipulation, hypnosis without any tricks. We listen to them because, next to them, we feel like losers.

'That's funny,' said Hervé, who had not resisted the temptation to read the manuscript before giving it to the publisher, 'because I've read it before too, only in a monastery.'

'So situating the action in a Sri Lankan prison is an original idea, I agree, but change the end, please. Because the moment we learn that the window looks out onto a wall – we've been expecting that since the third page of your story. And given that there are only four pages . . . that doesn't leave much space for suspense!'

Ajatashatru realised that this story, which had been born in his brain, had actually gestated in someone else's brain before him.

'Come up with another twist for the end,' Hervé suggested in a kind voice, saddened by the crestfallen expression on the debut novelist's face. 'Like . . . I don't know, we discover that the blind man is not actually blind. Or that he's not in prison, that it was all a dream.'

'That's too obvious and overused,' said the publisher. 'It needs an ending that no one will be expecting. But I'm sure our writer will find a wonderful idea. Won't you, *A-chattering-Hindu*? After all, he has quite a Maecenas behind him . . . Ah, Sophie, Sophie . . . But anyway, back to business . . . Perhaps this will inspire you?'

With these words, he took out a few sheets of paper.

'We are going to sign a contract today and you will have an advance so that you can work on the

217

book in the best possible conditions. Inspire us, Mr *A-jaunt-I-sat-through*. Did I pronounce that correctly?'

'An advance?' asked Ajatashatru, who could not have cared less how the man pronounced his name (badly, as it happened).

'Yes, money to cover your expenses while you finish the book. An advance on the sales royalties,' the handsome man explained. 'Do you have a bank account?'

'Um, no.'

'I thought as much. Which is why I took the liberty of anticipating . . .'

And, like a magician, he made a little black briefcase appear from under the table.

'All right, let's come to an agreement over the amount. How does fifty thousand euros sound?' the man said with a self-satisfied smile, his slender, tanned fingers drumming confidently on the black briefcase.

'Fifty thousand,' repeated Ajatashatru doubtfully.

The handsome *hidalgo*'s smile vanished.

'What? You don't think that's enough? All right, then . . . seventy thousand.'

The Indian said nothing.

'You're a tough negotiator, Mr *Ah-ha-I-have-you*! How about ninety thousand?'

Once again, the budding writer did not react at all.

'Well, well . . . who do you think you are, my little friend, J. K. Rowling?'

The former fakir's face lit up. 'J. K. Rowling? Isn't he some kind of magician?'

'She is a magician, yes. A magician who transforms words into gold. Oh, all right . . . One hundred thousand euros, and that's my last offer!'

'OK,' said Ajatashatru, unblinkingly.

A triumphant smile spread across the publisher's tanned face.

'Try not to look too thrilled! A hundred thousand euros for a first-time writer . . . and yes, you may be a genius who writes on his shirts, but you're still a first-time writer . . . well, personally, I think that's a pretty damn good advance. Anyway, I knew you would accept when it got to a hundred thousand. Which is why you will find that precise sum – not one euro less or more – in this briefcase.'

In fact, this little game might have gone on much longer, because our reformed fakir did not have the faintest idea how much money one hundred thousand euros really was, hence his apparent lack of reaction.

After a moment, he seemed to finally respond, and a broad smile appeared on his face. Surely this was enough money to buy an aeroplane ticket to Paris. And if there was any change left over, he could get a bouquet of flowers for Marie.

The man handed him the contract. Even though it was written in English, Ajatashatru signed it without even reading it, so excited was he at the prospect of going to see the Frenchwoman, a bouquet of flowers in his hand. Surprise!

'I'm glad you came to an agreement,' said Hervé. '*A-jack-an-ace-a-two*, all you have to do now is rework the ending of the book. As for the money, that is a lot of cash. Don't open the briefcase here – do it in your room, alone. The streets and hotels of Rome are not particularly safe. You'll have to put all of that money in the bank. We can take care of that for you this afternoon, if that's all right with you.'

The two men got up and left. Alone now, the Indian got up too, briefcase in hand, and approached the reception desk. Behind the counter, a digital display gave the real-time exchange rate of every currency in the world. That morning, one euro was worth exactly 6,782,800 Indian rupees.

The calculation did not take long.

'Six million seven hundred and eighty-two thousand eight hundred rupees!' Ajatashatru breathed, in his own language, hardly able to believe his eyes. 'Holy cow!'

With that much money, he wouldn't just be able to buy an aeroplane ticket and a bouquet of flowers, but the aeroplane itself, along with all its crew, and an entire florist's shop. Held to his chest at that moment was more money than he could hope to earn in ten reincarnations.

Keeping a very tight grip on the briefcase, he ran to the lift, unwittingly ignoring an astonished-looking Sophie Morceaux, who was waiting to eat lunch with him.

Ajatashatru Oghash Rathod had been pacing up and down his room for several minutes now, like a dog that cannot decide where it wants to sleep. His indecisiveness concerned where he might hide such a huge amount of money. Having been a thief himself, he knew that nowhere in the world was entirely secure, least of all an Italian hotel room, and that it would take no more than five minutes for any passing robber to find the briefcase stuffed full of cash and make off with it.

So he decided the wisest thing was not to let it out of his sight. In fact, safer still, he would not let it out of his touch. Yes, he was going to hold onto this briefcase for dear life.

He had taken a quick look inside the briefcase when he first got back to the room, just to make sure the money was real, and that he himself had not been conned and lied to. But no, it really was bursting at the seams with pretty purple notes. Genuine €500 notes, printed on both sides!

All right, so what should I do now? he wondered. He could hardly lug the briefcase around everywhere he went, even if that was the safest option. Sophie was waiting for him so they could eat lunch together. Perhaps it would be wiser if she came up and they ate in his room? Yes, that seemed the safest option.

He picked up the telephone, called reception and asked the employee to tell the pretty young woman who was reading in the lobby that she should go up to room 605.

Ten seconds later, there was a knock at the door.

Wow, that was fast!

'Hairdresser!' shouted a nasal voice from the other side of the door.

Unless she had suddenly caught a cold and changed her profession, it did not seem likely that this was Sophie Morceaux.

'Sorry?'

Ajatashatru was not entirely au fait with local customs, but he found it rather strange that a hotel, even an ultra-luxurious hotel like this one, would allow a hairdresser to offer their services in the corridors. And, anyway, everything seems strange and suspicious when you are holding a briefcase containing €100,000 in cash.

'No thanks.'

'You have to at least sign this paper to show that I've offered you the services.'

Sign a paper? That seemed serious. And surely he had nothing much to fear from a hairdresser . . .

'Where should I sign?' the Indian asked unsuspectingly as he opened the door.

'Where should you *die*?' he was corrected by a small, swarthy man, who blocked the door with his foot and pulled a flick knife from the pocket of his cheap trousers. Hairdressers aren't what they used to be.

Seeing the man's heavily scarred arms, the ex-fakir joked, 'Sorry, I've given up pain.' But his nonchalance was a bluff.

'I have a message from Gustavo,' the man said in heavily Italian-accented English.

His face, unusual physique and dress sense were all reminiscent, Ajatashatru thought, of the French taxi driver.

'*Just-a-mo*? Sorry, I don't know him. I'm Oghash.'

This reply did not seem to please the Italian, who

leapt forward, knife in hand. Ajatashatru jumped quickly backwards, allowing him to evade the blade but also allowing his attacker to enter the room. Remembering his fight in Barcelona, and in particular the ice cooler that had smashed him in the face, the Indian decided to try something similar, and he drove the briefcase hard into the Italian's nose, thus evening the score. The man's large head crashed noisily into the door of the wardrobe that stood at the side of the entrance hall.

The path to freedom was now clear. But only for a few seconds: the time it took the gypsy to recover from the blow. Ajatashatru did not hang around. He ran through the open doorway and hurtled down the emergency stairs as if he were being pursued by a guy who wanted to turn him into a sieve, which indeed he was.

Arriving in the hotel lobby, he passed the reception desk and sped towards the exit, once again failing to even notice the beautiful but rather surprised actress who was waiting to eat lunch with him.

At that moment, Sophie Morceaux was watching, open-mouthed, as Ajatashatru rushed from the hotel, carrying a briefcase. As Hervé had just told her the good news about the €100,000 advance, it seemed clear that her new friend had fled with the bread, made a dash with the cash, decided to go with the dough. This felt like a smack in the face to her. Sophie's concepts of friendship and trust had been dealt a severe blow. How could he do this to her? She had taken him in, given him a room, a handsome suit, her affection and her time. She had even found him a publisher merely by batting her eyelids.

She sighed. After all, this man was essentially just an illegal alien, a petty criminal. What did she expect? A leopard can't change its spots. She felt betrayed, thrown away like a used Kleenex, and she promised herself she would be more wary towards the next Indian who came out of her

Vuitton trunk. Enough was enough! In a rage, she threw her copy of *On Winter Mornings the Rabbits Yelp Lugubriously on the Road* by Angélique Dutoit Delamaison to the floor and went to shut herself up in her room.

At that moment, Gérard François was weaving his moped through Rome's nightmarish traffic. Tied to his luggage rack was the contract signed by the unusual writer. He could already see the best-selling novel stacked high on the shelves of the world's largest bookstores, and translated into thirty-two languages, including Ayapa Zoque, an ancient Mexican dialect spoken by only two people in the world, neither of whom could read.

At that moment, Ajatashatru was running towards the gardens he had seen from the window of his room. He had never run this fast in his life before. Particularly not while holding a briefcase containing €100,000.

At that moment, Hervé was in his room, swallowing the last mouthful of whisky from the minuscule bottle he had taken from the minibar. He was drinking to forget, but it wasn't working. Again, he thought about Gérard François's tanned complexion, his thick, moist lips. Why were his most handsome friends all heterosexual, handsome and, above all, friends?

At that moment, Gino, knife in hand and head still spinning slightly, was hurtling down the hotel's stairs in pursuit of the Indian who had stolen from and humiliated his cousin, and was now re-offending, at his expense this time.

At that moment, Ajatashatru was still running.

At that moment, Captain Aden Fik (who?), at the helm of his freight ship flying the Libyan flag, was skirting the Italian coast, glad to be on his way home after three months at sea.

At that moment, Gustave Palourde was deep in discussion, over a good garlic chicken – *un pollastre a l'ast* – with the father of the young Catalan baggage handler about the marriage that would unite their respective progeny, and therefore their families.

At that moment, Miranda-Jessica Palourde, soon to be Miranda-Jessica Tom Cruise-Jesús Palourde Cortés Santamaría, was putting a half-eaten chicken thigh back on her plate and greedily licking her fingers while eyeing her future husband, who was sitting across from her.

At that moment, Mercedes-Shayana Palourde

was shedding a few tears and deciding to give Sophie Morceaux's chic underwear to her daughter for her wedding night.

At that moment, Tom Cruise-Jesús Cortés Santamaría was lost in contemplation of his future wife, who was lasciviously licking her fingers as she ate a chicken thigh. Had he been Hindu, he would have had no hesitation choosing which animal he would like to be in his next incarnation.

At that moment, Ajatashatru wondered if he would ever stop running.

In Sanskrit, Ajatashatru means *He whose enemy is not born*. But he was really starting to put the lie to his name, given all the enemies he was accumulating.

When he lifted his eyes from the rough path on which he had been running since entering the Villa Borghese gardens, the Indian noticed that he was in the middle of a small, circular clearing.

He looked left, then right. Exposed and defence-less, he thought he was done for. But this was not the end of his race. A few yards ahead, taking advantage of the treeless area, the Italians had installed a huge hot-air balloon. It was blue, decorated with classical golden motifs. Just beneath it, attached by thin ropes like a thousand golden threads, a basket that was fixed to the ground shivered slightly in the wind. This was the first time that Ajatashatru had seen such a contraption in reality. He had seen one in the film *Five Weeks in a Balloon*, though, adapted from Jules Verne's novel of the same name.

When it was hoisted up over a hundred feet from the ground, this hot-air balloon provided tourists with a panoramic aerial view of the Roman capital for the modest sum of five euros.

As luck would have it, the basket was still on the ground, and a few tourists were queuing up to get in. There was no one inside at that moment, as the guide was very busy selling tickets.

Ajatashatru turned round. The gypsy was running towards him. He had put his knife away so as not to arouse suspicion, but the Indian was convinced that, once he got close enough, the fact that he was in full public view would not prevent him taking the knife out and running it through Ajatashatru as if the Rajasthani were a voodoo doll. Had he been performing one of his magic tricks, our ex-fakir might have been thrilled at such a prospect but, oddly enough, without a retractable blade and a few accomplices, the scenario lost much of its allure.

Without a second's hesitation, the Rajasthani leapt into the wire basket.

The guide saw him and shouted: 'Hey!'

The tourists saw him and gasped: 'Whoah!'

Gino saw him and yelled: 'Aha!'

Ajatashatru had been right. Regardless of all the witnesses, the gypsy pulled the flick knife from his pocket and held it in front of him, ready to deliver the final thrust. Only a wire basket now separated the Indian from the blade's sharp point. Utterly exhausted, Ajatashatru closed his eyes and bent down, his hands on his knees as he attempted to catch his breath. This is where my journey ends, he thought. The last thing he saw was the painting on the wall of his hotel room. All his dreams now were of peace and tranquillity. To his surprise, he found himself wishing that he could be reincarnated as a hay bale in a quiet field.

When Ajatashatru opened his eyes, he became aware that he was still alive and that he had not been transformed into a hay bale. His eyelids had shut just as the man had hurled his knife, blade first, at his stomach. But, instinctively, the Hindu had thrown himself backwards, tripping over an obstacle in the process and falling horizontally onto the cold floor of the basket.

He remained in this position for a few seconds, finding it considerably more comfortable than standing face to face with a murderer ready to do him in for €100 and perhaps nick a briefcase from him containing €100,000. This was the second time in two days that he had used the 'playing dead' technique. It was starting to become habit, a genuine combat strategy.

After a few minutes passed without the gypsy, the guide or any of the tourists climbing into the basket, Ajatashatru sat up and looked around him, speechless. He realised that the thing he had tripped over was in fact a large ice cooler and that there were other objects on the floor, including a handle that opened a trapdoor and yellow carboys that undoubtedly contained reserves of gas.

The Indian climbed carefully to his knees and took a look through the holes in the wire basket. The hit man had vanished, along with the guide and all the tourists. Everything had vanished: the trees surrounding the clearing in the gardens, the gardens themselves, the houses, the hotel, Rome, the Earth . . . everything. Around the basket, as far as the eye could see, there was only powder-blue wallpaper decorated with little white marks. The sky.

The hot-air balloon had liberated itself from its shackles and, free for the first time in its long career in tourism, had risen into the air, leaving terra firma forever.

The writer leaned over the side a little bit. Below him hung the rope that, a few minutes earlier, had held the machine fast to the ground, and that someone had cut through with a knife. He was not dead, but was that a good thing, now that he found himself abandoned in the infinity of the firmament and at the mercy of a diabolical contraption that he had no idea how to work? Wasn't this only a temporary reprieve before a death that was just as inevitable and far crueller than being repeatedly stabbed with a knife on solid ground?

The Parisian taxi driver was not humane enough to wish his enemy a speedy death. He had probably ordered the hired killer to provide the Indian with a slow and painful end. And, spotting the balloon, the hit man had seen his chance to inflict the most vicious torture imaginable.

Ajatashatru did not suffer from airsickness or vertigo, thankfully, but seeing the houses as small as those plastic ones in Monopoly and the tourists as tiny as ants in sandals was enough to throw even the most Zen of Buddhists into a panic.

Had there been no wind, the balloon would simply have hovered over the clearing in the Villa Borghese gardens. Instead, it drifted slowly but surely towards an unknown destination, carried away by Aeolus's breath. It was now at an altitude of five hundred feet, and from there our hero could see the city limits, the fields surrounding Rome and some silvery reflections in the distance. It was towards those pearly flashes that the balloon was flying, at about ten miles per hour. Soon, Rome would be nothing but a memory, a tiny dot on the horizon. Yet another city that I won't get to explore, thought Ajatashatru.

Above the Indian, the canvas globe gaped open like the mouth of a yawning octopus. In *Five Weeks in a Balloon*, he had seen that a wheel had to be manipulated occasionally in order to send flames or gas up inside the balloon. This worked on the principle of hot air rising above cold air, carrying the balloon with it. So he looked for the wheel, found it and turned it. Like an angry dragon, the fuel reserves breathed gigantic flames, which disappeared inside the darkness of the deep throat.

A hot-air balloon cannot be steered any more now than it could two centuries earlier. It drifts wherever the wind takes it. Its pilot knows where he is taking off from, but not where he will land. That is the whole appeal of ballooning.

Although the average length of a balloon flight is around sixty minutes, one can, depending on the amount of gas available, remain airborne for as long as two or three hours, sometimes even longer. A balloon generally travels between six and twelve miles in an hour, so it did not take more than three

hours for Ajatashatru to reach the Mediterranean
– which was, of course, the very moment chosen
by the gas reserves to run out and for the contraption to begin its inevitable descent towards the deep
waters of the sea.

The ex-fakir could do nothing to ward off fate.
All he could do was watch helplessly as the balloon
fell towards the threatening surface of the water.
This was it, then: he was going to die. Drowned,
because he had never learned to swim. Then again,
what good would it have done him even if he could
swim? The coast moved ever farther from view with
each passing second. He would try a few clumsy
breaststrokes, and then he would sink inexorably,
like a stone, to the bottom of the sea.

So his journey ended here. All that, just for this.

The pretty blue surface was his finishing line. But
the pretty blue would soon change to puma red,
and then to blood red. So, there was something
worse than the syndrome of the truck that slowed
down and stopped: the syndrome of the balloon
that slowed down and fell into the sea.

Pulling himself together, he looked around for a
life jacket but could not find one, because of course
the balloon was not intended to do anything other

than rise and fall in the same fixed place above Rome. Inside the ice cooler that he had tripped over, he found some cans of soda, useless in these particular circumstances. He tried opening the trapdoor, then almost fainted when he looked down into the void. He immediately closed it again and waited, resigned to his fate.

He waited until the basket landed on the water and began to sink. Around him, the vast sea stretched out in all directions. In a few minutes, he would be trapped underwater inside a wire cage. In a few minutes, he would be dead. Ajatashatru Oghash Rathod would vanish from the surface of the Earth. His final disappearing act.

He looked out at the vast blueness. How many lives had been lost here? Fishermen, lone sailors, pilots who had run out of fuel, illegal aliens freezing on stowaway ships, all those hundreds of African illegals that Assefa had told him about who disappeared each year between Libya and the Italian coast without ever having reached the promised land, their only mistake to have been born on the wrong side of the Mediterranean. So, there you go, he would die like them, dragged under by the cold water. One more body for the insatiable killer.

And then he realised that, if he died now, the world would remember him only as a con man, a thief, an egotist, someone who devoted his life to taking from others without ever giving anything in return. Was he ready to face the final judgement with this weighing on his conscience? Your CV is not exactly great, Buddha would say, playing with his long earlobes.

No, he could not die. Not yet.

Not before he'd been able to help someone. Not before he had shown – to others, and to himself – that he had changed.

And then, there was Marie. He could not die before he had ever known love. That would be ridiculous.

In the space of a few seconds, his entire conversation with the Frenchwoman flooded back into his memory like a film played on fast-forward, and then he saw his cousin and his adoptive mother, all the happy moments he had experienced in their company, and then he remembered the less happy moments: the hunger, the violence, those men leaning over him and drooling, those clammy hands gripping him, those snakes biting him. His whole life passed before his eyes. A short life, so eventful but so vain. No, there was no way he could meet Buddha like this. He would undoubtedly be re-incarnated as a cherry tomato on a skewer, a fate very different from the tranquillity of being a hay bale in a quiet field.

But what could he do in order to avoid death? The situation did not seem very promising. He was a prisoner in a trap that was closing around him a little more with each passing second. Ajatashatru knelt down in the basket, which was already leaking water, and held the briefcase tight to his chest. The briefcase which was stuffed with money that would now be of no use to him whatsoever. As if to prove, for once, the truth of the saying 'Money can't buy happiness'.

Captain Aden Fik had never seen a buoy as big and blue and as far from the coast as the one he was seeing now from his pilot house. So, being an enlightened and pragmatic man, he came to the conclusion that it was not a buoy.

But what was it, then?

A weather balloon that had fallen from the sky? The mushroom from Tintin's fantastic island? A hot-air balloon whose basket contained an Indian and a briefcase stuffed with €100,000 in cash?

Whatever it was, it was something strange and unusual, and that did not bode well. It could easily be a trap laid by pirates. He turned up the engine, propelling his freight ship forward more quickly.

Aden picked up his binoculars and examined the UFO (unidentified floating object). Straight away, he realised it was a hot-air balloon. But where the basket should have been, there was only the opaque surface of the sea. It looked as if the basket had been completely submerged, along with its occupants.

Dismissing the possibility that this was a trap laid by pirates, the captain called one of his officers and ordered him to put a lifeboat out to sea with two men, so they could take a closer look at it. He had to act fast. Aden would much rather pick up the living than the dead. You could always get something from a living person. The dead were worthless.

Twenty minutes later, the men came back in the lifeboat, accompanied by a tall Indian, thin and gnarled like a tree – a wet tree, in this case – and wearing a white turban. With one hand, he held onto the aluminium survival blanket that had been draped over his shoulders; with the other, he gripped tightly to a black briefcase that he seemed reluctant to let go.

'I am the captain of this vessel,' Aden Fik announced proudly in English, relieved to have found a living person from whom he might be able to squeeze something. 'It was lucky for you we were passing at the right time. What happened to you?'

Ajatashatru introduced himself and explained that he had been taking part in a hot-air balloon race near Rome when an unfavourable wind had made him deviate dangerously from his course towards the sea. When his gas reserves ran out, his only solution had been to land on the water. He would have drowned if the captain's men had not appeared.

'In that case, welcome to the *Malevil*. I imagine your most pressing desire is to return to Rome and get back to your normal life,' added the captain, ogling the survivor's mysterious little black brief-case. 'However, due to a tight schedule, it is impossible for me to go back to the Italian coast. You are therefore obliged to swim there, which might prove rather difficult with a briefcase in your hand, or to stay with us until we reach our final destination, Mr *I-shat-a-satchel*. But in that case, you must pay. As I'm sure you're aware, life has a price. Unlike death . . .'

These words made Aja shiver. Yet again, it seemed he had flown from a frying pan into the fire. Perhaps he should have drowned when he had the chance?

'And where are we heading to?' he asked, forcing himself not to show the fear he felt.

But his hand was shaking so violently against his briefcase now that it was audible. He sounded like a Brazilian percussionist during carnival season in Rio.

The captain pointed to the red, black and green insignia sewn onto his shirt. 'To Libya, of course! Now, tell me what you have in that expensive-looking briefcase . . .'

Libya

When the *Malevil* dropped anchor in the port of Tripoli the next day at 2 p.m., Ajatashatru walked down the pontoon that led him to solid ground, €15,000 lighter than he had been before, but relieved.

The forced crossing had proved expensive. It could have been much worse, however. On the ship, he had been at the mercy of the Libyans' moods. After all, the captain could have taken all his money and thrown him overboard, without anyone knowing. Yes, he had definitely got off lightly.

Libya was going through a period of unprecedented unrest and everyone wanted money, even captains of freight ships. Particularly captains of freight ships, in fact. To make ends meet, they sometimes transported illegal aliens, from Africa or elsewhere, towards Italy. On occasion, when an Italian patrol was drawing close, the traffickers would throw the illegals in the water, whether they knew how to swim or not. That way, the Italians were forced to rescue them and to take them to the coast, while the criminals could sail back to Libya, unpunished and undisturbed, to plan the next crossing.

Nine months after Colonel Gaddafi was overthrown by NATO forces, the country was still the victim of terrible violence, rape and unending human rights violations. So you have to feel some compassion for those poor people. When they were given the opportunity to save an Indian and his briefcase containing €100,000 from the middle of the sea, they weren't going to let him go scot-free. Obviously he was going to have to make a contribution towards the welfare of Libyan citizens who were living through one of the darkest periods in their history.

But in that case, you might ask, how did our Indian manage to save himself for a mere €15,000 when he was carrying a briefcase that contained €100,000?

Well . . . when you know how to transform water into wine using dye capsules skilfully hidden in the palm of your hand, when you know how to twist 'thermomolten' metal forks simply by looking at them and stroking them, when you know how to stab a skewer in a false tongue that you are holding between your teeth, you are in a good position to escape – with a little intelligence – from any sticky situation or excrement-filled creek in which you might find yourself.

So when the captain, holding a pistol, had politely asked Ajatashatru to open his briefcase, the ship-wrecked Indian could find nothing to reproach in the request and accordingly did as he was told.

A purple haze – the colour of the €500 notes – lit up the Libyan's face, like the face of a pirate who has discovered treasure.

'I rather doubt you fell into the sea during an innocent hot-air balloon race, Mr *I-ingest-ash-atchoo!* In fact, I suspect you were trying to escape from someone. The police, perhaps. Did you rob a bank?'

'Don't get too excited. These are counterfeit notes,' Ajatashatru told him persuasively. He had stopped trembling and now seemed to have the situation in hand, because he had thought of an idea.

'They look pretty genuine for counterfeit notes!' said the captain, who was not going to be outfoxed by someone who was even more of a crook than he was.

'That's because they're well done. All of this is equipment for a magic show. It's worthless, I swear on my integrity as a fakir!'

With these words, Ajatashatru took a half-dollar coin from his pocket and tossed it in the air.

'Heads,' he bet.

And the coin did indeed fall into the palm of his hand, face side up.

'All right, heads again,' said the Indian, tossing the coin in the air for a second time.

Once again, he won his bet.

'I know this trick,' said the sailor confidently. 'It all depends how you toss the coin.'

'Close,' said Ajatashatru, showing him the half-dollar's two identical sides. 'But no cigar! People often think magicians have great talents for manipulation when the whole secret lies in their equipment . . . Another demonstration?'

The Indian did not wait for the captain to reply. He dug into his trouser pocket again and pulled out his green €100 note. He turned it over several times in his hand, showing the front and the back.

'So?' said the Libyan, bored with this little magic show.

'So what do you see?'

'A one-hundred-euro note.'

'Well observed. And does it seem normal to you?'

'Yes, completely normal. Well, as far as I can tell, anyway. You keep turning it over like an omelette.'

'Wrong again,' Ajatashatru told him, opening wide his Coca-Cola eyes.

The captain looked startled.

'Contrary to what I told you a minute ago, rigged equipment is not always enough, in itself, to create an illusion. So, the magician has to use all his talents as a conjuror.'

And, with these words, he slowly turned over the note to reveal the blank underside.

'That note is only printed on one side! But I . . . that's impossible!' stuttered the captain, unable to believe his eyes.

'Just a question of training,' said the fakir/writer, turning the note over with a click of his fingers and this time revealing that the side which had been blank was now printed.

'Incredible . . . How do you do that?'

The magician went on without listening: 'As for

this briefcase, it's rigged. It looks like it is full of notes – real ones – but that, I'm afraid, with all the respect due to a man who is pointing a pistol at me, is purely in your head.'

Ajatashatru took a purple note from one of the wads in the briefcase, held it out in front of him, his fingertips touching the upper corners, as if he wished to admire the watermark, and began to methodically fold it in two, then in four, then in eight, and so on, until the piece of paper was no bigger than a fingernail. He blew on his two hands and the note disappeared. Then he took another note from the wad and did the same thing, three times running.

'You see, these notes do not exist,' said Ajatashatru, lifting his hands in the air so that the three folded-up notes in his sleeve could fall down inside his shirt. 'They are magic notes. Which really just means fake notes.'

'I don't understand,' admitted the man, beginning to take the bait.

'It's very simple. These notes are made from unleavened bread, a one hundred per cent organic product with no yeast and no sugar,' the fakir lied. 'The same procedure as for Catholic priests' wafers, basically. The notes melt in my hands, which are warmer than the air in the room, and they vanish without a trace.'

'Amazing!'

'So that is why, although I appear to be in possession of a vast fortune, I cannot pay for my journey, captain, because this pile of cash is just a mirage, an illusion. And a tasty one, into the bargain.'

Unfortunately for Ajatashatru, Captain Aden Fik was a big food lover. So, in the end, the price paid by the shipwrecked Indian for crossing the Mediterranean was three purple millefeuilles, which were in reality three wads of €500 notes, amounting to a grand total of €15,000. It could have been worse, though: had the fakir not used his famous gift of the gab to preach the benefits of a balanced diet and to warn about the outrageously high calorie content of unleavened bread, the captain would have taken the entire briefcase.

So that was why, as soon as the *Malevil* dropped anchor in the port of Tripoli the next day at 2 p.m., Ajatashatru ran down the pontoon as quickly as possible and disappeared into the quayside crowds. He was imagining the Libyan's face when he started chewing his money and discovered that it did not melt in his mouth, and particularly when he realised that these were real notes, and that he had let slip a briefcase stuffed full of cash.

The Indian found himself in the middle of a mosaic of unfamiliar smells and colours that reminded him how alone he was here. For a moment, he felt homesick for his village, his loved ones, his ordinary daily life. These days spent in strange lands were beginning to weigh heavily on him.

In this part of the world, people had olive skin just as they did in his country. But they did not wear turbans or moustaches, and that made them look younger. There were also a lot of black people like Assefa, eyes full of hope, who appeared to be waiting for boats to take them to that yearned-for continent of Europe, which he had just left so easily. Around them, men – some dressed in military uniform, others in civilian clothes, but all of them carrying machine guns – walked around smoking contraband cigarettes, to remind you that you were on the wrong side of the Mediterranean.

In his posh suit, incongruous amid the local dress code of tracksuit and sandals, Ajatashatru attempted not to draw too much attention to himself. In the last twenty-four hours, he had already been threatened with an ice cooler, a knife and a pistol. As the weapons wielded by his enemies seemed to be exponentially increasing in power, he might soon, if he wasn't careful, find himself staring down the barrel of a rusty old machine gun. So the magician became, for a little while, a small beige-coloured mouse, scurrying towards what it thought was the way out of the port while carrying a brief-case containing €85,000.

When it arrived at the guard post, the little Indian mouse found itself looking on helplessly as two soldiers, armed to the teeth, took advantage of a young black man. One of the soldiers had slammed the foreigner against a wall and the other one, cigar-ette dangling from his mouth, was nonchalantly going through his pockets. They took the little cash that they found, as well as his passport. They would get a decent sum for that on the black market. Then the soldiers spat on the ground and went back to their sentry box, laughing loudly.

The young man, robbed of his identity and the small amount of money he'd had to pay for his crossing to Italy, slid hopelessly down the wall like a hunted animal that is so badly wounded it no longer has the strength to stand upright. When his arse touched the dusty ground, he buried his head between his knees to disappear from this hell.

A chill ran down Ajatashatru's spine. Had he not, in his banker's suit, been as conspicuous as the Great Wall of China on Google Earth, he would have knelt down next to the poor man and helped him to get up again. But it was better not to draw more attention to himself. Yes, he would have knelt down next to him and talked to him about Italy or France; he would have told the African that the journey was worth all the difficulties. That he, Ajatashatru, had friends in the same situation, who must, at that moment, have been jumping into a truck bound for England, their pockets stuffed with chocolate biscuits bought in France, from a supermarket where there seemed to be so many things in abundance, all within reach for the price of just a few banknotes printed on both sides. That he had to keep going, not to give up; that the promised land was there, on the other side of the sea, a few hours' journey in a hot-air balloon. That, over there, there were people who would help him. That the 'good countries' were a box of chocolates, and that the most likely scenario was not that he would be greeted by the police. And that, even if he was, the police there did not hit you with big sticks, like they did in Ajatashatru's village. There were good guys everywhere.

But he would also want to tell the young African that life was too precious to be risked, and that it would do him no good to reach Europe dead, whether drowned in the sea, or asphyxiated in a cramped hiding place inside a delivery van, or poisoned in the tank of a fuel truck. The Indian thought again about a story told to him by Assefa, about some Chinese people that the police had found piled ten high in the seven-square-foot false ceiling of a bus, all of them wearing incontinence nappies to piss in. And some Eritreans who had been forced to call the police themselves with a mobile phone because they were suffocating inside a truck, having been locked in there by a human trafficker. Because for the traffickers, who made money from the vulnerability of migrants, all that mattered was the price. A price that could range from €2,000 to €10,000, depending on which border was being crossed. They were paid for the result, and so, as the result was that the migrant reached their destination, it didn't really matter whether they did so whole or chopped into little pieces, or whether the first thing they saw in the good country was a hospital room. If they were lucky.

Ajatashatru remembered how he had felt when he fell into the sea in his hot-air balloon: the fear of dying alone and anonymous, of never being found, of vanishing from the surface of the Earth under a single wave, like being erased from a page, just like that. The young black man almost certainly had a family waiting for him somewhere, on this continent, on this side of the great divide. He could not die. He must not die.

The Indian wanted to say all of this to him. But he didn't. The crowds of people had stopped looking at the young man and were going about their business like ants. Ajatashatru glanced towards the sentry box. The soldiers were still laughing heartily inside their fish bowl. If they didn't rob him, it would be the captain who had brought him here who would soon come rushing from his ship like a fury, his eyes filled with hate and greed, giving the signal to all the mercenaries who were hanging around here – and Buddha knew there were plenty of them! He could not stay here.

Ajatashatru took out one of the €500 notes that he

had kept in his pocket and walked straight towards the guard post. On the way, he brushed past the young black man and let the note fall to the ground next to him, whispering 'Good luck' into his beard, though the young man surely didn't hear him.

But he'd done it. He had helped someone. His first human. And it had been disconcertingly easy.

Having achieved this, Ajatashatru was overcome by a feeling of well-being, as if a radiant little vapour cloud had appeared inside his chest, and was spreading throughout his body, to the end of each limb. Soon, the cloud enveloped him completely and Ajatashatru felt as if he were floating up from the dusty ground of Tripoli's harbour on an enormous and extremely comfortable armchair. It was easily the best levitation he had ever performed. And it was also the fifth electric shock he received to his heart during this adventure.

He would have risen into the Libyan sky, above the border patrol and the barbed-wire fence of the port, if, at that moment, a loud voice had not hailed him from behind. Startled, he fell back to Earth with a bump.

It took Ajatashatru a few seconds to react.

Behind his back, the voice spoke again.

'Hey!'

This is it, I'm really done for now, the Indian thought. The ship's captain must have sent his henchmen after me. His heart began to bang like a tambourine inside his chest. What should he do? Turn round as if everything were fine? Ignore the voice and run like crazy towards the exit? They would catch him easily.

'Hey, Aja!'

At first, the Indian thought he must have misheard.

'Oh gosh!'

Ajatashatru turned his head slowly. Who was this person who knew not only his first name but his second name too?

'Aja, don't be scared – it's me!'

Finally, the writer recognised that cavernous

voice that he had heard for the first time through the door of a wardrobe in a swaying truck. That powerful voice which had told him all its owner's secrets without even trembling.

It was really him.

It was Assefa.

Ajatashatru was almost in tears. His lips stretched into a wide smile and the two men leapt into each other's arms.

It was with mixed feelings that he saw his friend again. On the one hand, the Indian was happy to finally see a familiar face in a part of the world where everything was strange. But on the other hand, if Assefa was here, that meant he was not in Spain, or in France, that he was not about to cross the border into England as he had imagined. And that made the Indian sad.

'Ajatashatru, you have an amazing knack for turning up where I don't expect to see you!' exclaimed the big African, ending their hug with a pat on the shoulder.

'The world is a handkerchief, as the Spanish say. An Indian silk handkerchief.'

'It seems as if things are going well for you,' said Assefa, nodding at the Indian's new suit and his briefcase. 'You look like a wealthy Indian industrial-ist. Where did you come from?'

Ajatashatru pointed to the *Malevil*.

'That ship is coming from Italy!' Assefa said, baffled. 'Aren't you going in the wrong direction?'

The ex-fakir explained for the third time in his life that, unlike Assefa, he was not an illegal alien and he was not attempting to reach England.

'Listen,' he said to the African, who was looking at him sceptically, 'I owed you an explanation in the truck. For reasons that you know about, I wasn't able to tell you my story. But now, fate has brought us back together, and I think the moment has come.'

'*Mektoub*,' said Assefa. 'It was written.'

The two men sat at a table in a seedy bar in the port area, sipping warm beer and taking refuge from the soldiers and the tumultuous chaos of the city, and had a heart-to-heart.

Having left Barcelona, Assefa, who was now travelling alone, had been retracing his footsteps, at the mercy of international readmission agreements. He had been sent flying from country to country as if he were a grenade with the pin removed. First Algeria, then Tunisia, and finally Libya. Which was a little odd, as he had not been through any of these countries on his original journey. But whatever . . . All that mattered to the authorities was to pass this problem on to someone else as quickly as possible. You might even say that they had succeeded in inventing their gigantic immigrant catapult.

The African, who would never give up – because going back to Sudan empty-handed would be not only an immense humiliation and a personal failure, but also a flagrant waste of money for his village, which had gone into debt to pay for his journey – was now getting ready to cross the Mediterranean again for the small Italian island of Lampedusa. It was so frustrating when you thought about it! Only a few days before, he had been standing in the promised land of Great Britain. He had got there. If only the police hadn't stopped that damn truck . . .

'But, you know, there's always someone worse off than you. During one of those repatriation flights, I talked with a Chinese guy who told me how they had to pay an astronomical amount to get to Europe by plane, with high-quality false passports, and when they reached France they had to work all day and all night in illegal sweatshops in a Paris suburb to pay back their trafficker. And because the Chinese place so much importance on the culture of respect, they don't even try to escape, they don't say 'Up yours' and run away. They would lose face and it would be a great humiliation for them not to pay back the cost of their passage. It's a sort of moral obligation. So they sit down at their sewing machines and work. Apart from the pretty girls, who are not so lucky. The girls are locked away in filthy apartments and forced to prostitute themselves to pay for their journey to this heaven, which soon turns out to be a short cut to hell.'

Assefa said all of this, apparently unaware that the same thing happens to young African girls.

'So, you see, there's always someone worse off,' he concluded. 'White, black, yellow . . . all of us are in the same boat.'

'I don't know who is the worst off, Assefa, but I'm pretty sure most white people are not in the same boat.'

'So what about you, Aja? I want to hear your story now.'

The Indian swallowed a mouthful of warm beer and, as they had plenty of time, began at the beginning.

'I was born between the tenth and the fifteenth of January 1974 (no one knows the exact date) in Jaipur, in India. My mother died giving birth to me. A life for a life. That is often the price of a baby for someone from a poor family. My father, incapable of looking after a kid on his own, sent me to live with his sister, the mother of my favourite cousin Parthasarathy (who is like a brother to me). My aunt, Fuldawa (pronounced *Fold-away*), lived in the little village of Kishanyogoor, on the border with Pakistan, in the desert of Tharthar. That is where I grew up, in the middle of nowhere. But my aunt thought of me as one more mouth to feed rather than a real member of the family, so she did everything she could to make me feel unwanted. That's why I was always holed up with the next-door neighbour, Adishree, who raised me like I was her own son. It can't have been easy for her. I was a wild child, although also curious and affectionate. Lulled by the tales she invented for me, I dreamed about becoming a writer or a storyteller myself. At the time, we hardly had enough to eat. We had no money. We lived like cavemen. One day, an Englishman who was passing through – a geologist who was studying the Tharthar Desert; the only guy I've ever met who was interested in a pile of sand – showed me a cigarette lighter, and gave it to me in exchange for a blow job. Back then, I had no idea what a cigarette lighter was, never mind a blow job. I was only nine years old. I did eventually learn what it was, and that it was bad. But I had already been thoroughly abused by then. Anyway, the Englishman made little sparks burst from his thumb, and I found that magical. A beautiful blue flame appeared, there in the middle of the desert. He could see that I was interested in the object. "You want it, don't you?" he asked me. And that was how I found myself on my hands and knees between his legs, doing something I didn't understand, happy at the thought that I would receive this magical object in return. I sucked a guy off for a cigarette lighter! Can you believe it? A fucking lighter! And I was just a kid. That makes me want to throw up. So, anyway, one blow job later, I ran off to show the lighter to my friends. You always have a feeling of superiority when you perform a magic trick. Simply because you are the only one who knows the secret. And because people admire you. That feeling quickly becomes an addiction, believe me. Me, a poor kid from the desert, being admired . . . can you imagine? And so I became a fakir. I was so good at ripping off the people in town, especially the intelligent ones! Because intelligent people are easier to fool. They are sure of themselves, so they don't pay attention. They think nobody can make a fool of them. And, just like that, you've got 'em! Their self-confidence is their undoing. It's different with the idiots. They're used to people thinking they're stupid, so as soon as they come across a smooth talker, they're immediately on their guard. They analyse all your movements. They never let you out of their sight. They don't let anything go. And so, paradoxically, it is much harder to confuse them. Robert-Houdin said that. A French magician. And he was right. But, anyway, during my adolescence, I lived for a while with a venerable Rajasthani yogi. I learned everything from him. The art of eating packs of fifty-two cards (I was a difficult kid: I only ever ate Bicycle-brand cards), of walking on cinders and broken glass, of piercing my body with kitchen utensils, and providing my master with good blow jobs, as instructed. I concluded that this was just the standard way of showing your appreciation to grown-ups. I devoured every book written on the subject (magic, I mean, not blow jobs): Houdini, Robert-Houdin, Thurston, Maskelyne. I made a rope dance with the sound of my flute, then climbed up it and disappeared in a cloud of smoke. I was so skilful that people soon came to believe I had supernatural powers. I became a demigod in the village. If only they'd known . . . In reality, my only power was to avoid being found out! But, anyway, my reputation took me, at the age of twenty-five, to the golden palace of the maharaja Abhimanyu

Ashanta Nhoi, where I was hired as a fakir and jester. My job was to entertain the court. By any means necessary. So I lived a life of falsehood and trickery. And that trickery soon turned against me. I had to play the part, you see. As it was much more spectacular to claim that I lived on a diet of rusty screws and nails, rather than ordinary food, well, that was all they gave me to eat. I was dying of hunger. I lasted a week. One day, unable to take it any more, I stole a few bits of food from the kitchen and devoured them in secret. They caught me red-handed. The maharaja was appalled. Not because I had stolen, but because I had lied. I had taken him for a fool, basically, and that was difficult for a man of his rank to accept. First they shaved off my moustache, the supreme humiliation, and then the maharaja asked me to choose between teaching schoolchildren about the perils of theft and crime, or having my right hand cut off. 'After all, a fakir fears neither pain or death,' he said to me with a big smile. Naturally, I opted for the first solution. To thank him for giving me a choice of punishment, I offered him a blow job. My intention was wholly innocent. Wasn't this how adults were thanked? Nobody had told me it was bad. I was still a virgin. Outraged, he literally kicked me out of the palace. I understand that now. When I think about it, I feel ashamed. Penniless, I began working as a wandering con man. I cheated everyone: my own people, tourists, everyone I saw. Recently, I made everyone believe that it was essential for me to buy the latest bed of nails from Ikea. And they all fell for it! I could have told them I was going off to find the Golden Fleece. The whole village contributed. Of course, I don't sleep on a bed of nails. I have a nice, cosy bed hidden in a wardrobe in my living room. But I thought I could sell it afterwards. Perhaps it was just a whim, I don't know, or perhaps I just wanted to see how far those gullible idiots would go to pay for anything I wanted. The village went into debt for me, just like yours did for you, Assefa. But with me, it was just trickery. Selfishness. I didn't want to help anyone. People I had known since childhood gave me money when they didn't even have enough to eat. All in the hope of helping me, helping this demigod I had become. But this journey has changed me. I am no longer the same person. First there was your story, which moved me deeply, and there have been other encounters, caused by the unexpected events that have marked my journey: finding love with Marie (I'll tell you later), making friends with Sophie (ditto). And then the eighty-five thousand euros in this briefcase. Hang on, don't look at me like that, Assefa, I'm going to tell you about that too.'

After telling him in detail about the latest events in his life, Ajatashatru downed the rest of his warm beer and gazed at Assefa with his Coca-Cola eyes. His friend did not speak, did not know what to think. The story had blown him away. What if the Indian's apparent desire to redeem himself was just another trick, another lie?

Ajatashatru looked at the briefcase, then at his Sudanese friend, and then at the briefcase again. He felt sure about this. Finally, he had found the right person to help. It was obvious. He thought again about the African's long journey, which seemed as endless as his own.

He also remembered the feeling of well-being he had experienced when he gave the €500 note to the young immigrant in the port, the radiant cloud that had spread through his body and enveloped him in an ethereal haze. His heart beat like a tambourine. He had discovered that there was a stronger, better feeling than the arrogant satisfaction of having taken something from someone through cunning and deception: that of giving something to someone who needed it. The young African in the port had been his trial run; now it was time to perform his masterstroke.

Ajatashatru glanced furtively around him. They were sitting in an isolated corner of the bar. There were only two other customers anyway, in fact: two old sea dogs speaking in their own language, telling one another of their adventures. They clinked their glasses loudly together, perhaps to celebrate the fact that they were still alive after a whole lifetime spent defying the waves and the tides.

The Indian opened his briefcase, picked out several wads of cash, counted them and placed them in front of his Sudanese friend.

'That is for you, Assefa. It's for your family. Forty thousand euros.'

He closed the briefcase.

'What's left in this briefcase is for my family: everyone I've cheated, dishonoured, deceived. Forty-five thousand euros to redeem myself, so they have enough to eat, so that they can live like human beings.'

Assefa's jaw hung open. To begin with, he had not really believed the story about the French publisher in Rome, the novel written on a shirt, the manuscript, the advance, but he had to face facts. How else could the Rajasthani have got so much money?

'With that much money,' Assefa mumbled, 'I wouldn't even need to go to England. Do you understand, Aja? I could go home to Sudan, to my family, without any worries . . .' He had said this with a glimmer of homesickness in his eyes. 'But I can't accept it.'

Ajatashatru had thought the feeling of well-being produced by the act of giving would be proportional to the sum given. So he was expecting it to be eighty times more powerful than the feeling that had come over him when he dropped that €500 note next to the young African who had been so foully robbed. But it didn't work like that. It was not the amount you gave that counted, but simply the gesture of giving. He had felt the same emotion as the previous time, with the same amount of power. His cloud had lifted him from the table and up towards the ceiling of the bar. But Assefa's last sentence was a bombshell for Ajatashatru, and once again he came back down to Earth with a bump.

'You have to accept! I am not leaving with that money. It's yours, Assefa – take it!'

'It's your money. You earned it honestly – *for once* – by writing your book.'

'Well, exactly. If it's mine, I'm free to do whatever I like with it.'

Ajatashatru would never have believed it could be so difficult for an illegal alien to accept €40,000 in large bills.

'Do it for me, Assefa. No more ships' holds, no more car boots, no more goods lorries. I want you to be a free man, not a hunted man living in constant fear. A man catapulted from country to country. Be a father again, Assefa. Your children are waiting for you.'

Assefa hesitated for a long time – about two seconds – and then accepted.

Banknotes, like pigs, sleep alternately: one pointing up, one pointing down, one pointing up, one pointing down. That was how Aja arranged the wads of purple notes that remained in his briefcase.

The two men had gone their separate ways – one heading north, the other south – but they would never forget the times they had shared. Perhaps, one day, their paths would cross again? *Mektoub*. Perhaps it was written? The world was a real Indian silk handkerchief.

The Indian writer sat in the back seat of a taxi, headed towards the airport. The last taxi he had taken had, in a sense, been the starting point for this extraordinary adventure. This one – the seats of which were far less comfortable but the driver of which was, at least, not trying to kill him – would mark the end.

The decision had been made. The Indian would take the first plane for Paris, he would see Marie

again, agree to have a drink with her or to go and
buy lamps in Ikea, he would not withdraw his hand
when she touched it, and he would spend his
evenings watching her beautiful curled eyelashes
batting in rhythm with his heart. He would show
her all the magic tricks she wanted and he would
rewrite the ending of his novel, with his beloved's
head leaning on his shoulder.

He had nothing left to do in Libya. Well, in truth,
he had never had anything to do in Libya; he had
been like an oak that one day found itself replanted
in the Sahara Desert. But most of all, he had nothing
left to do in India. The new Ajatashatru Oghash
Rathod did not belong there. Like the cobras that
he had spent his career charming, he had shed his
skin. He had left the skin of an old con man back in
Kishanyogoor. He could not return and admit that
his life up to this point had been one big charade.
He could not give back the hope that he had stolen
from his people. They would not understand. Even
if he did return, he was no longer a fakir. He had
never had any special powers. That had just been a
way of separating you from your money, of cheating
you out of your meagre savings. He could not change
water into wine, he could not cure cancer, and he

was too squeamish even to give blood, never mind stick a fork in his tongue! Oh, but you saw him do it? Yes, but that was a latex tongue!

No, seriously, he could not go back. He had to begin a new life elsewhere, far from there. In a country where there was no risk of him ever bumping into anyone from his Tharthar village. He would call Parthasarathy and Adishree as soon as he arrived and explain the situation to them. They would be upset, of course, but they would understand. He would send them €35,000. For them and for the village, so that they would never be in need again. They would really understand then. He would keep €10,000 for himself – for himself and Marie, rather, because he would now have to start thinking for two. The money would be their flying carpet, allowing them to take off for a new life.

An honest, innocent, normal life.

And there would be love in it, too. He was sure of that.

But when he arrived at Tripoli International Airport, the plans he had made collapsed like a house of (rigged) cards. The last plane for Roissy Charles de Gaulle had left the day before, and the next one was not due for two days, possibly more, depending on how long it took to remove the latest rebels who had taken over the runway.

In the old days, Hindus had used their turbans to measure the depth of wells. For the first time in years, Ajatashatru took his off in order to measure the depth of his sorrow.

It took longer than expected to liberate the two tarmac runways of Tripoli International Airport. He had to wait five days. Five seemingly endless days during which he remained holed up in his hotel room, only leaving occasionally in order to buy food. You have no appetite when you are in love. And even less appetite when you are in love in a war-torn country. He did not want anything more than packets of crisps, bars of chocolate and a few boiled sweets. Oh, and some nice hot baths.

You're probably thinking that, with all that money in his briefcase, he could have eaten in the best restaurants in the Libyan capital, so why stay for five days in an airport hotel? Well, quite simply, because the city's chaotic atmosphere did not exactly encourage foreigners to walk through its streets, pockets stuffed with cash, in search of a five-star restaurant. There were hardly any tanks in the roads now, that was true, and the army no longer forced foreigners to board large fishing boats and sent them off to the Italian coast, as they had been doing a few months before, but still . . . it wasn't Euro Disney either. And what Ajatashatru Oghash Rathod had seen in the port of Tripoli would remain engraved in his memory for a long time. The young African sliding down the wall to weep with rage after he had been robbed by the soldiers. Had he noticed the banknote? What had he done with it? Where was he now? Questions that would forever remain unanswered, but to which the Indian preferred to give optimistic responses.

And so the vending machine in the airport a few floors below his hotel was emptied, day after day.

Cut off from the rest of the world, as if he had washed up on a deserted island, the Indian had plenty of time to think over his recent experiences. The wacky race that had brought him here. The strange events that had made him a new man. The five electric shocks he had suffered during his journey. When you have spent your whole life living frugally and then you suddenly find yourself carrying a briefcase that contains €100,000, you quickly turn into a philosopher.

When he had first received the money, he had

been mistrustful because if there was one thing life had taught him it was that gifts did not simply fall from the sky like that, no strings attached. Not unless you gave a blow job or two, anyway. The world was full of con men, cheats and bastards, just like him. The world was a vast hunting ground. And he knew what he was talking about because he himself had been one of the predators.

But when he had seen his hotel room in Rome, such luxury given without anything being asked in return, and then all those purple banknotes just for a few lines written on a shirt, he had realised just how good man can be. People had simply trusted him. Like Sophie Morceaux, actress and inter-national star, who had given some of her time to look after him and help him. He had to thank her, and explain the reasons for his precipitous depart-ure. He would write her a long letter as soon as he got to Paris.

So, the world was not filled only with con men, cheats and bastards. And his recent encounters had taught him that there was something much more valuable than fraudulently taking money from people: giving away that money, and spreading goodness all around. Had he heard this from someone else, he would have found it fake and sugar-coated, sickeningly sentimental, ridiculously utopian. But it was so true. He remembered the look on Assefa's face when he had given him the €40,000. It would be a while before he forgot those eyes. Or Marie's.

Marie.

Soon.

Each night, he fell asleep thinking of her, to the sound of machine-gun fire. As he slept, the briefcase that he held tightly in his arms was transformed into the Frenchwoman's slender body, plunging him into the most wonderful of dreams.

France

The day before his departure, Ajatashatru called Marie from a public telephone box and told her about his imminent arrival in Paris and his resolutions. To make her his. Never again to withdraw his hand when she touched it, never again to reject the offer of a drink with her or a romantic evening. He wanted to go with her to see his cousins, who sold Eiffel Towers and apartments on the Champ de Mars. He wanted to see everything with her.

'You know, the funniest thing about all this is that you've been to England, to Paris, to Barcelona, to Rome, and you have never seen Big Ben or the Eiffel Tower or the Sagrada Familia or the Colosseum or anything like that. You're a bit like my friend Adeline, who knows the most famous capitals in Europe only by their airports. She's a flight attendant. But never mind, you and I will go together and I'll show you the "good countries".'

She had used Assefa's expression, and Ajatashatru

could not help but wonder where his friend was at that moment. Not on his way to Europe, at least, sitting on the dusty floor of a truck. Would the money be enough to ensure that his children no longer looked like they were hiding a balloon under the skin of their bellies, that the flies would never again hover around their lips, that their country and their eyes would shine once again? Would it be enough to ensure that they could think of something other than hunger?

'We've already lost enough time,' said Marie, bringing him back from his thoughts.

'Yes,' he replied.

His eyes sparkled, and so did his ears.

Can you imagine how Marie felt when she hung up? She was over the moon, of course! She felt like she was twenty again. She put on her trainers and ran out to buy scented candles, duck breasts and four nice yellow apples.

Happy are those who, like Ajatashatru Oghash Rathod, have made an incredible journey in a ward-robe and then returned, older and wiser, to live with his beloved for the rest of his life . . .

Whoah, hang on a minute! Don't speak too soon, thought the Indian, sitting in the comfortable seat of the Airbus that was carrying him towards Paris. Given my luck so far, it's not out of the question that this plane will be diverted. And then, before I know it, I'll be back on the roller coaster again! I won't be able to rest easy until I've landed in Paris and I am holding Marie in my arms. He took a quick look at the pretty bouquet of white daisies that he had placed on the empty seat next to him.

Then, suddenly imagining a gang of terrorists, armed to the teeth, getting up and taking control of the aeroplane to redirect it towards Beirut or some other exotic destination, Ajatashatru glanced furtively around him, looking for bearded men in turbans wearing sticks of dynamite in their belts. But, very quickly, he realised that he was the only bearded man in a turban on this aircraft. A terrorist – that was, perhaps, what all the other passengers were thinking at that moment, after all.

If only they knew. He was a lord now, a true maharaja, his turban spick and span so that his beloved would like it. Rich in his heart, and rich in his briefcase too. And he was entering France through the front door. In the seat of an aeroplane too – a rather original mode of transport for this man who had, in recent times, been more used to travelling in an Ikea wardrobe, a Vuitton trunk or a hot-air balloon. He was no longer, however unwittingly, an illegal alien. The curse had finally been lifted. When he thought about it, he had been lucky. He had made an extraordinary nine-day journey, a voyage within himself during which he had learned that, by discovering all the other things that existed elsewhere, he could become someone else.

The day he had helped the young African and Assefa in the port of Tripoli, he had given more than he had ever given in his life. And not only financially, although €40,500 was undeniably a very large sum of money, a fortune. He remembered with delight the feeling of well-being that had filled him on those two occasions, the comfortable cloud that had lifted him higher than any of the mechanisms he had used for his magic tricks. Now he wondered who would be next on the list. Which person in need would he help next?

The steward announced that the aeroplane was beginning its descent, and that everyone had to ensure their seat and table were in the upright position and that all electronic devices were switched off.

Ajatashatru sat up and slid his feet into his shoes, along with – unknown to him – a very thin contact lens that had stuck to his socks while he was tenderly rubbing them on the sumptuous carpet.

He felt as if he were going home.

Marie was his home.

He thought about the very nice welcoming committee that awaited him at the airport in Paris. His little Frenchwoman. Who could ask for more?

At that moment, a beautiful Frenchwoman wearing a turquoise dress and silver-coloured sandals was excitedly getting into a small, dented red Mercedes with Gypsy Taxis painted on the front doors. From its stereo she could hear a lively tune played on the guitar by the Gipsy Kings.

'Charles de Gaulle Airport, please. Arrivals lounge. I'm going to meet someone who is landing in half an hour, coming from Tripoli. That's in Libya. The war-torn country. Well, the country that used to be war-torn, anyway.'

The driver nodded impatiently to say that he had understood, that there was no need for so many explanations. He was a fat man with a tuft of salt-and-pepper chest hairs emerging from his open-necked black shirt. His pudgy fingers, decorated with gold rings, gripped the steering wheel as if he were ready to make a quick getaway at any moment.

On the dashboard, a taxi driver's licence with a black-and-white photograph indicated that the man's name was Gustave Palourde, that he was a pure-blooded gypsy, and that his number was 45828.

'Why are there bouquets of flowers stuck to the doors?' Marie asked.

This is going to be a long journey, thought Gustave, who was already imagining his customer with an Indian zip on her mouth.

Annoyed, he explained: 'My daughter is getting married tomorrow.'

His fingers drummed out a castanet solo on the steering wheel.

'Congratulations!' the woman exclaimed. 'You must be so proud and happy!'

The driver hesitated for a moment.

'It's a good match, yeah.'

'Oh, don't say that! Isn't your daughter marrying for love?'

'Palourdes don't marry for love, madame; we marry for the good of the family. Love comes later. Or not, as the case may be . . .'

'And you're working until the day before the wedding!' Marie observed, to steer the conversation into less dangerous waters.

'I have to earn the money to pay for the couple's new caravan.'

'I understand,' said the Frenchwoman, who did not understand.

How could people camp all their lives, and voluntarily too? It was difficult to grasp for Marie, who had never in her life stooped to sleeping anywhere but in a large, comfortable bed. Not even on a sofa.

'Where is the groom from?'

'He's Spanish.'

'From where?'

'He's from Barcelona,' said Gustave testily, then continued before the woman could ask him another question: 'He's going to come and live here, in Paris, in our community. That was the agreement. It's usually the wife who follows her husband, but in the Palourde family it's the women who decide. And me. The kid comes from a big gypsy family in Barcelona. I'm glad our blood lines will be mixed.'

'A mixed marriage,' said Marie, watching the road thoughtfully. 'Mixing is so wonderful. Actually, as we're on that subject, the person I'm meeting at the airport is not French. He's my fiancé.' She did not feel she was lying when she said this, only anticipating. 'He's Indian. With a little luck, we'll be celebrating a mixed marriage too, one day . . .'

What on earth had got into her to think things like that? And to say things like that? People really did like to confide in strangers.

Marie continued to stare at an imaginary point on the road ahead of her, somewhere between the two headrests. She imagined herself with Ajatashatru, wearing a nice sari, surrounded by bright colours, rose petals thrown at their feet as they passed. A real princess.

'Indian . . .' repeated the driver, who also looked thoughtful. 'To be perfectly honest, madame, I have no great love for Indians.'

Saying this, Gustave let go of the steering wheel with his right hand so he could caress the ivory-handled Opinel knife that never left the front pocket of his trousers.

'I knew one who was a very bad person. A thief. And, let me tell you, if our paths ever cross again, I will make him suffer for his sins . . .'

'Oh, you mustn't generalise. They're not all like that,' said Marie, who held back from mentioning that many people had the same opinion of gypsies. 'Mine is an honest man. A writer.'

'A writer?' said the taxi driver, who had never read anything other than street maps of Paris.

'I would be honoured to introduce him to you. Would you wait for me, when we get to the airport? That way, I won't have to find another taxi and you will get to meet Ajatashatru. I can't wait to introduce him to you. He will change your opinion of Indians, I'm sure.'

'That is all I ask, dear lady.'

The flower-covered Mercedes sped along the motorway. The sun was slowly setting, painting the trees and buildings orange.

The taxi driver slapped himself on the forehead, then looked at his watch.

'You know what? It actually works out well that you're going to the airport. My cousin Gino is arriving from Rome. I didn't think I'd be able to pick him up. He's coming for my daughter's wedding. He's going to do her hair. So if you don't mind, while you go to pick up your boyfriend, I'll pick up Gino and we can all meet back at the taxi. What do you think? Would it bother you to share a taxi with my cousin?'

'Oh no, of course not!' Marie exclaimed delightedly. 'Quite the contrary. The more the merrier!'

Little did she know just how true this would prove.

CHAPTER THREE

As Devanampiya collapsed suddenly on the cold, damp floor of the prison, Walid asked another prisoner what was happening and learned that his friend was dead.

So Walid cried. (I checked: blind people do cry.) He cried his heart out that night. His sobs could be heard as far away as his home, in Afghanistan.

He had lost a friend, his only friend, and with him, he had also lost the ability to see. Under these circumstances, prison would soon become a hell again.

CHAPTER FOUR

When Walid woke up that afternoon, he was surrounded by three doctors. Had he not been blind, he would have seen that the grey, filthy walls of his cell were now white, shiny walls. The floor was so clean that you could eat off it. And it was full of medical equipment, making it look more like a hospital room than a prison cell.

The blind man attempted to sit up. A hand pushed him back down while a loud voice spoke to him in a language he did not understand but which he identified as being Sinhala.

He wanted to ask what was happening, but when he opened his mouth he noticed that there was a tube inside it that prevented him from speaking.

Another series of incomprehensible sounds ordered him not to move or tire himself out.

Walid lay back down without asking any questions, his mind tormented by the confusing situation, until, a few hours later, an Afghan interpreter was sent to his bedside and the tube removed.

The patient could now communicate with his doctors.

'What is your name?'

'Walid Nadjib.'

'Good,' said the doctor, as if he had been verifying something he already knew. 'I am Dr Devanampiya. Do you know where you are at this moment?'

Devanampiya? Walid was dumbstruck. He did

not understand. Then again, perhaps it was a common name in these parts?

'In prison,' he muttered.

'In prison?'

Apparently, this was not the correct answer.

'You are in Colombo Military Hospital.'

'What am I doing here?' Walid asked fearfully. 'Am I ill?'

He remembered the devastating death of his friend when he came back from his walk. Had he suffered the same fate?

'You are the only survivor of a terrorist attack. There was a large explosion on the aeroplane you took. A 747 heading to London. In all likelihood, a suicide bomber managed to make his way through security with a fairly powerful explosive device. When you were found amid the debris, you were in a terrible state, let me tell you. You were in a coma for two months and we really thought it was all over for you. But, a few hours ago, you woke up. It's a miracle, in my opinion. One of the most devastating attacks of the century. Two hundred and eighteen dead, and only one survivor.'

No matter how hard he tried, the blind man could not remember a thing. Or rather, his memories did not correspond at all with what the doctor was telling him, as if he had been living a parallel life up until that moment. What he remembered was the police arresting him just after he got through security, then the prison in Colombo, then Devanampiya's death. But now he learned that all of this had been merely a figment of his imagination, a coma dream. He discovered – from the mouths of people who had no suspicions at all, particularly not of a poor blind man who had survived a terrorist attack – that his mission had succeeded. As to why he wasn't dead when the explosives had been hidden inside his white cane, he had no idea. Perhaps a steward had taken it from him while he helped him onto the aeroplane, and then forgotten to give it back to him? Whatever the truth of this, Walid thanked his lucky stars and wept with joy, demonstrating that blind people can indeed cry.

Impossible, thought Aja. I cannot possibly end my novel like that. I can't conclude this book in such a horrible way. The killer cannot triumph. This ending might well be more original than the other one, but that doesn't alter the fact that it's bad, very bad. And, above all, immoral.

Immorality was a new concept for him.

He screwed the three pages into a ball and threw them in the metal bucket under the table. The budding writer did not know the tricks of writing a good story, but in the few books he had read that were not about prestidigitation, he had noticed that, no matter how dark or hard the stories were, they usually finished with a happy ending, a hint of hope. As if the story were a long dark tunnel and the last page the light at the end.

Perhaps he would quite simply never manage to rewrite the ending of his novel. Perhaps he did not deserve the €100,000 they had given him and the trust they had put in him.

This story of the blind terrorist: he had no idea where it had come from. But the character was not like him at all, or at least it was not at all like the man he was now. He wanted the story in his book to provide some hope, if only out of respect for the wonderful people he had met during his adventure. Those men and women, black and white, Sophie and Assefa and all the others, what they had in common was a big heart. So why not tell the story of that fabulous journey which had changed him forever? It was a true story, too, not an invention. It was *his* story. It was what had made him the man he was today. Not only that, but it finished well. He had found a woman and a new family: the true happy ending. The kind of light that shone brightly after the long dark tunnel of his life.

Next he considered a title, because he thought this was how novels were started. 'What do you think of *The Extraordinary Journey of the Fakir Who Got Trapped in an Ikea Wardrobe?*' he wondered aloud, as if the little dog from the aeroplane hold was there, witnessing the birth of his new book. He imagined it barking three times to encourage him.

This title summed up his story nicely. The story of Ajatashatru Oghash Rathod, man of the world, formerly a fakir, now a writer, the man who discovered Europe in an unusual way, by wardrobe, trunk, hot-air balloon, ship and baggage carousel.

He thought for a few moments.

When he finally came up with the first sentence of his new novel – *The first word spoken by the Indian man Ajatashatru Oghash Rathod upon his arrival in France was, oddly enough, a Swedish word* – he glanced out of the window and grinned happily, that satisfied smile that great men make when they know they are on their way to achieving great things. Then he gingerly touched the large bandage that covered his ribs, took a deep breath and left the caravan.

The sounds of guitar music, shouting and casta-nets assailed his ears. For a brief moment, he thought the nightmare that had so disturbed him in Italy had come to life. He saw himself trans-formed into a chopped (holy) cow, roasting on the end of a skewer with his cousin turned into a cherry tomato, turning round and round over the fire to the music of the Gipsy Kings. The horror!

He leaned against the caravan door. His heart felt as if it were going to burst out of his chest.

'What have you been up to?' asked an Indian princess, who turned out to be Marie dressed in a green tunic.

Relieved not to be a (holy) cow roasted medium-rare, Ajatashatru let go of the door, leaned on the arm of his beloved, and walked with her towards the multicoloured crowd.

'Nothing. I was just writing. I had an idea, and I wanted to get it down before I forgot it.'

'No writing today. Today, we celebrate!'

With these words, the Frenchwoman kissed him, then took his hand and danced a few steps of a flamenco. Next to her, a young blonde gypsy girl dressed in a hot-pink wedding dress slammed the wooden heels of her shoes on a table.

At that moment, a fat-bellied man dropped his guitar, got up and came towards the Indian. When he was close enough not to be heard by anyone else, he whispered to him: 'No hard feelings, eh, *I-had-to-slash-you*? I hope you're not angry with me for that little knife wound.'

He put his hand on the Indian's ribs. Even without an ice cooler in his hand, Gustave Palourde remained a threatening presence.

'But don't forget our agreement, *gorgio*. If you hadn't promised to amuse the kids with your magic tricks, even this handsome €500 note wouldn't have stopped me turning you into an Indian sieve, you know . . .'

As Marie was watching them from a few feet away, happy and tipsy and utterly carefree, Ajatashatru felt obliged to smile. He looked around until he found the children, took a deep breath, and pushed his way through the crowd.

Not long after Miranda-Jessica and Tom Cruise-Jesús's wedding, Ajatashatru proposed to his beloved after a romantic meal at *Métamorphose*, an old barge moored on the Seine that had been transformed into a restaurant and cabaret with a magic show. With the aid of the local illusionist – a man who had mixed with the most famous people on Earth and whose face smiled out from posters all over the boat – he made an engagement ring appear on a little Indian silk handkerchief, which was carried by a mechanical butterfly with yellow-and-blue wings and dropped delicately onto Marie's shoulder. The Indian remake of an 1845 trick by magician and watchmaker Robert-Houdin.

During the meal, and before the Frenchwoman discovered to her amazement the beautiful ring hidden inside the handkerchief, the two lovers had shared a little of their intimacy – at least in their thoughts – with their family and friends.

Ajatashatru's four favourite cousins (in order of preference: Parthasarathy, Ghanashyam, Nysatkharee and Pakmaan) and Adishree, with whom the couple regularly kept in touch, were planning to come and visit them soon in their little Montmartre apartment. Perhaps they would stay and become estate agents in Paris. The Eiffel Tower was still for sale, after all.

The global success of Ajatashatru's book had enabled Assefa to track down the Indian exile and write him a letter to congratulate him and thank him once again for his generosity. With the money, they had built a school in Assefa's village and rescued several families from poverty and hunger. The flies remained, however: there was nothing to be done about them.

Now that Sophie Morceaux had discovered the truth behind Ajatashatru's actions, she was no longer angry with her friend for running off with a briefcase full of cash and not even a word of goodbye. The two of them now shared the same manager, Hervé, whose hands were as clammy as always.

Ajatashatru was no longer just a man who wrote stories. Having quickly developed a taste for helping others – addicted as he was to the cloud of pleasure that lifted him high into the sky whenever he performed good deeds – he had, with the aid of Marie and the huge royalties he had earned from his book, set up an association that welcomed and helped those most in need.

Ikea's designers, moved by what Ajatashatru had been through in the truck that took him to England, had started work on a brand-new model of wardrobe complete with a toilet and a survival kit. It would undoubtedly prove to be their best-selling item in the coming months on the Greek-Turkish border.

Finally, the lovers talked about the latest shipwreck: the boat that had disappeared with seventy-six migrants on board, somewhere between Libya and Italy. At that moment, several Guárdia di Finanza helicopters were flying over the Mediterranean in search of the ship. Despite the best efforts of the rescuers, they would never find it, nor would they find the lifeless body of a young Somalian – a seventeen-year-old boy called Ismael – who had boarded the ship one morning, full of hope, after Allah had given him a sign by dropping a €500 note at his feet, enabling him to pay for his crossing.

During that candlelit dinner, 854 migrants would attempt to illegally cross the borders into the 'good countries' so that they too could enjoy that wonderful box of chocolates. Only thirty-one of them would make it, with fear in their guts when the truck slowed down but did not stop.

To this day, Officer Simpson has not discovered a single other illegal alien hidden inside an Ikea wardrobe. This is perhaps because his boss, having read Ajatashatru Oghash Rathod's novel and discovered his innocence, had promoted Rajha Simpson to a position as crossing-keeper at the docks in Dover. The police officer's most notable activity is now throwing dried bread to the seagulls, which he hopes will soon become an Olympic discipline.

Marie said yes, of course.

Kneeling in front of her, Ajatashatru slipped the pretty engagement ring onto her finger. Then he stood up and gave her a long, passionate kiss as everyone smiled and applauded. A few days later, a famous Indian dressmaker in the Passage Brady in Paris took Marie's measurements so he could create a sumptuous red-and-gold sari for her.

The car that will take her from Montmartre to

the Hindu temple has already been reserved. It is an old red Mercedes, slightly dented, with a bunch of Ikea saucepans tied to its bumper. Their clinking and clanking will be heard all the way to the distant starlit dunes of the Tharthar Desert.

SAM TAYLOR is a translator, novelist and journalist. His translated works include Laurent Binet's *HHhH* and Joël Dicker's *The Truth About the Harry Quebert Affair*. His own novels have been translated into ten languages.

www.vintage-books.co.uk